ACCIDENTALLY PREGNANT!

ACCIDENTALLY PREGNANT!

BY

REBECCA WINTERS

First published in Great Britain 2010
Large Print edition 2011
Harlequin Mills & Boon Limited,
Eton House, 18-24 Paradise Road,
Richmond, Surrey TW9 1SR

ISBN: 978 0 263 22172 5

Harlequin Mills & Boon policy is to use papers that are
natural, renewable and recyclable products and made
from wood grown in sustainable forests. The logging and
manufacturing process conform to the legal environmental
regulations of the country of origin.

Printed and bound in Great Britain
by CPI Antony Rowe, Chippenham, Wiltshire

CHAPTER ONE

Greek CEO of the Simonides Corporation, Andreas Simonides, thirty-three, astonished the corporate world by marrying unknown, twenty-six-year-old American, Gabriella Turner, in a private ceremony on Milos.

THE AUGUST HEADLINES in the *Corriere della Sera* caught Vincenzo Antonello by the throat. While in town he'd bought a newspaper before stopping off for lunch, never dreaming what he'd read when he opened it. In a gut reaction, his hands gripped the edges of his Italian newspaper so tightly, it started to tear down the middle.

"Papa? Are you mad?" His six-year-old son had stopped eating his pasta salad to stare at his father.

"No." Vincenzo caught himself in time. "It tore by accident."

"Oh. Can we go to the park now and play soccer?"

"In a minute, Dino. Let me finish my coffee first."

Sources close to the Simonides family have closed ranks on the press, but one rumor has floated that the elusive couple are honeymooning in the Caribbean and won't be available for pictures or comments for some time to come.

The CEO's former Greek girlfriend, Irena Liapis, daughter of Athenian newspaper magnate Giorgios Liapis, was expected to become the bride of the brilliant Simonides tycoon. Since the surprise announcement, it has been learned that the twenty-seven-year-old Ms. Liapis, who heads the monthly lifestyle section of her father's newspaper, has resigned her position and dropped off the scene. Her location is unknown at this time.

An icy hand seemed to squeeze Vincenzo's lungs until he couldn't breathe. Since early July when Irena had returned to Greece, he'd honored her wishes by not going after her. Every day he'd expected to hear that she and the great Simonides were married.

When Vincenzo had first met her, he'd damned the man's very existence and had baited Irena constantly about her alleged feelings for the man she intended to marry. Those feelings had not stopped her spending one blissful night with him, though, Vincenzo thought angrily. He had hoped and believed that the night had been earthshaking for her, too, and that it had erased her desire for Vincenzo's nemesis.

But these headlines proved he'd only been deluding himself. Somehow he'd thought this was the one female on the planet who'd been different.

"Irena!"

"I know it surprises you to see me."

Deline hugged her. "Only because I thought

you'd already left for Italy. Why didn't you phone that you were still in Athens?"

"I—I didn't dare," she stammered.

"Not dare?" Her best friend's brown eyes looked at her with concern. "Come in and we'll talk." Irena moved inside. "I just finished feeding the twins. They're out in the garden room in their swings. Leon will be sorry he missed you. He left for work a few minutes ago."

"I know that, too. I came earlier and purposely waited until I saw his car disappear."

Deline had been guiding her through the Simonides villa, but after hearing that comment she spun around and put a hand on Irena's arm. "The minute I saw your face I could see something was terribly wrong. What is it that is troubling you, Irena?"

"My biggest fear right now is that your house staff will know I stopped by and mention it to Leon. *He just can't know I came here!*"

Unspoken words flowed between them. Deline was already reading between the lines and realized that whatever had brought Irena to the villa, it was deadly serious.

"The maids won't be in until this afternoon. The only person around at the moment is my housekeeper, Sofia. I'll find her right now and tell her that your visit is to remain private. She is a valued staff member and can be trusted, I'm sure. However, I will make it clear that if any of the staff or my husband hear about you having come over, she'll be in serious trouble."

No one ever had a better friend. "Thank you, Deline." They hugged again.

"I'll be right back."

As she darted away, Irena walked into the garden room. The five-month-old twins were in their swings facing each other. Each had a plastic toy and seemed perfectly content, but when they saw Irena, their little arms and legs started moving faster in excitement.

Irena knelt down next to Kris, who'd come through his heart surgery so well, you'd never know he was barely out of the hospital. She kissed his cheek, then turned to Nikos. Both beautiful black-haired boys had been made in Leon's image. Most people would assume Deline was their mother due to her black hair and olive skin.

But others who knew the Simonides clan well were aware of Leon's slip during a rough spot in their marriage. It had been a one-night mistake in a state of inebriation with Thea Turner, a Greek-American woman, now deceased, that had produced his beautiful children.

Incredibly, Deline, who was pregnant with Leon's child, had loved him enough to forgive him and take him back. They were now a family of four with another baby on the way.

"Problem taken care of," she announced as she hurried back in the room.

If only that were true...

"Tell me what's wrong," Deline begged after sitting on the sofa.

Irena eyed her dear friend who would have been her sister-in-law if fate hadn't stepped in to change lives.

Overnight, nothing was the same as it had

been before. Leon's twin brother, Andreas, was the man Irena had thought she would be marrying. But two months ago she'd gone to Cinque Terre in Italy for her job and had met another man. So strong was the attraction and feelings between them, she hadn't wanted to leave him.

When she had returned to Greece to tell Andreas the truth, he had been unavailable because of some mysterious circumstance. Irena had soon learned that Thea's half sister, Gabi Turner, had appeared on the scene and Andreas had taken one look at her and had broken it off with Irena. The next thing she knew Andreas had married the blonde American woman and had just left on his honeymoon.

"Irena Liapis— Talk to me!"

Her body started to shake. "I don't know how to tell you this."

"What?"

"You're not going to believe it. *I* don't believe it."

"It's that bad?"

"Much worse."

"Are you dying?"

Irena knew it was a serious question. "No, but at least it would solve my problem."

Without warning Deline jumped to her feet. "That's *never* a solution!" she scolded. "I was about to say that unless an incurable disease is about to take your life, nothing else you could tell me would rival what I've lived through while I decided whether to stay with Leon or not."

"Try this. *I'm* pregnant."

Deline paled. "Andreas's baby…"

After a brief pause; "Probably," she answered in a shaky voice.

Her friend's eyes widened with incredulity. "What do you mean probably?"

"The doctor worked out the dates with me. He's ninety percent sure it's Andreas's, but it could be another's. Oh, Deline, what if it's Vincenzo's baby?"

"Who's Vincenzo?" Her friend's loss of color

alarmed her so much, she guided her back to the couch where they could both sit.

"Vincenzo is a man I spent all my time with when I was in Italy doing my article for the paper. He is handsome and… Oh, what a mess!" Irena let her head drop into her hands, a sudden feeling of despair washing over her.

"How long have you known you were pregnant?"

"I've felt queasy for the last week and finally went to the E.R. yesterday. I thought maybe I'd come down with flu or something. The doctor there referred me to an ob-gyn who confirmed it this morning before I came here. I'm six weeks along."

She'd begged the doctor to go over the dates again…and again. When she'd left Greece for her newspaper assignment in Italy, she'd only slept with Andreas, the man she had assumed she would marry on her return to Greece.

But those ten days in Italy had changed the course of her life forever. There she'd met Vincenzo, had been hit hard and fast with feelings she had never experienced or felt before. So much so that she'd extended her stay to be with him and hadn't wanted to go back to Greece…or Andreas.

Her friend's eyes filled with tears. "Oh, Irena. No matter what, you're going to have a precious baby."

"I know." Moisture glazed Irena's cheeks. "I want it more than anything in the world." Wanted it to be Vincenzo's…she added silently.

"Of course you do." Deline squeezed her arm gently. "What are you going to do?"

Irena took a deep breath. "I know one thing I'm *not* going to do. Andreas will never learn the child I'm carrying is his, if it *is* his. I'm going to another OB this afternoon to get a second opinion. I *have* to be sure."

"I was just going to suggest that you see another doctor. This is too important."

"Oh, Deline…I want so much for Vincenzo to be the father."

"But if the next doctor tells you the same thing—"

"If he does, I still refuse to hurt Andreas and Gabi. You and Leon had to live through a nightmare when he came to you with the news that he'd fathered Thea's twins. I don't want to start another nightmare for them. They're in love. Andreas couldn't marry her fast enough. They're on their honeymoon making plans for their future. I won't do that to them."

Deline sat there shaking her head in disbelief.

"I want to be on *my* honeymoon with Vincenzo. I want to be able to tell him I'm carrying *his* baby. Sometimes I wonder how you got through it, Deline. I was so crushed for you." The twins were adorable, but they should have been Deline and Leon's.

"I'll never forget you were there for me." Her voice shook.

"I don't mean to bring up the past to hurt you. I just can't do that to them."

Deline got to her feet. "The truth has a way

of coming out, Irena. What if everything had remained a secret until years down the road? I'm not so sure our marriage could have withstood such a blow then. At least we're starting out with the truth now, before our own baby is born. And Leon has been so good to me— incredibly kind and understanding. Patient, you know?"

Irena understood. "Believe me, I'm thankful things are working out for you so well. But think, Deline— Maybe Gabi is pregnant already. I'm afraid of history repeating itself."

Her friend groaned.

"Wouldn't *my* news be a lovely belated wedding present for the two of them after they get back from the Caribbean… I can't do it to them."

"One day he'll find out, and when he does…" Deline actually trembled. "I know Andreas. Leon's brother is noble to a fault and he'll always care about you, but if you were to keep knowledge of that kind away from him and then he discovered it—especially after what he went through to make sure Leon was united with his own children—" She shook her head again. "I'd fear for you, Irena."

Put that way, so did Irena. She cleared her throat. "There's one way to handle it so he never finds out. That's what I came over to talk to you about."

"What? Move to another planet?"

"Not quite so far away. After I returned from Italy, I resigned my job at the newspaper. My plan had been to break it off with Andreas before I went back to Riomaggiore to be with Vincenzo. That's where I'm going now. What I'm hoping is that he meant what he said and still wants to marry me."

"Still? You mean in ten days you got to a point that he asked you?" Deline cried out aghast. "Not that you aren't the most beautiful and intelligent woman I've ever known. Any man would want you, but if he knew about Andreas—"

"It sounds complicated, I know. He didn't exactly ask. It more or less came out. But when

I left, I couldn't give him an answer until I'd talked to Andreas first, and you know what happened next. He was totally involved with Gabi!

"When he told me about her, it struck me then that Andreas and I had never been in love, otherwise Gabi couldn't have stolen his heart any more than Vincenzo could have stolen mine. Vincenzo warned me that if I'd gone through with that marriage, it wouldn't have worked, that one day I would regret my mistake—he was right."

Deline stared at her before an odd expression broke out on her face. "What kind of a man could have caused you to fall for him so completely in a ten-day period, you want to marry him and wish it was his baby you're carrying?"

Irena averted her eyes.

"Come on. Out with it."

"His name is Vincenzo Antonello. He's an irreverent bachelor who's Italian down to the roots of his hair." Curly, untamed, overly long black hair. "He either walks or drives his used Fiat if he has to go any distance." Irena smiled at the memory, so different from her life where she had grown up in a world of luxury villas, elegant cars, limo service and helicopters.

"He was assigned to give me and my photographer a tour of the liqueur manufacturing plant in La Spezia where he works. As he was putting me back in his car, he said he liked it that at five foot eight, I was closer to him in height. 'There's more to grab hold of.'"

His deep laughter had rumbled out of him along with the words spoken in heavily accented English. Insufferable, arrogant, but with those blue eyes piercing you through black lashes.

"Our whole meeting was absolutely crazy, Deline. The whole time I was there, he spent every waking hour with me. We laughed and ate and walked and talked. I've never talked with anyone else so much in my whole life. I don't think either of us got any sleep.

"We hiked, we played, we strolled. He bought

me flowers and little gifts. I was showered with them. He…bewitched me."

Six feet of proud, hard-muscled male, handsome as the devil he mocked. The antithesis of political correctness.

Irena had grown up cautious.

He was a Catholic, albeit not a good one, he'd admitted with a rakish white smile. She didn't espouse one particular religion. Irena believed in the emancipated woman who could be powerful in the corporate world.

"He has an opinion on everything and isn't afraid to express it."

No worshipper of money, Vincenzo. As long as he made enough at his job, he was happy to let someone else handle the financial nightmare of being a CEO. Irena came from a monied background. Her parents' very existence was defined by wealth.

"Vincenzo went out of his way to show me his village. Our walks in the hills took all day because he kept pulling me down to kiss me. On my last night there I ended up at his apartment in Riomaggiore. It was very small and simply furnished. He fixed me an Italian meal to die for.

"We drank wine and danced on his veranda until it got dark. When he picked me up and carried me to his bedroom, it seemed entirely natural. I'd stopped thinking because these overwhelming feelings had taken over. Before I flew back to Greece, he said something totally ridiculous to me."

"What was that?" Deline had been watching and listening, spellbound.

"'We are opposites in every conceivable way, Signorina Liapis. I think we should get married.'"

"Irena—"

"He shocked me, too. He enjoyed doing it on a regular basis."

"What did you say to him?"

"From the beginning he knew how things stood with me, that I'd loved Andreas Simonides for a long time and expected to be his wife soon."

"How did he handle that?"

"He laughed at me. 'Love? If you two truly loved each other, you would be married by now and not here with me.'"

Irena bowed her head. "I have to tell you, Deline. Those words pierced me because I realized he was speaking the truth. Andreas and I had been drifting. If I'd felt for him what I felt for Vincenzo, I wouldn't have let my career take precedence over being with him whenever possible.

"Vincenzo kept firing truths at me. 'What is love, anyway? A word. It can mean anything you want it to mean at the moment. Then again it can mean nothing at all.'

"I asked him if he didn't believe in it. He shrugged his shoulders and did that Italian thing with his hands and arms. Then he said, '"I believe in forms of it. Who couldn't love a child, for instance?"'

"When I told him he was impossible to talk to, he said, 'Why? Because I don't conform to your misguided idea of perfection or feed you what you're used to consuming? Have you ever taken a good look at yourself?'"

Deline shook her head. "I can't believe he dared."

"He dared more than that. 'Ms. Liapis,' he said. 'You are like the geese that fly in chevron formation—cool and unflappable, you cruise above the world with your fine-feathered family unit as you were taught to do, careful not to be diverted by other species of birds or natural disasters.'

"'But I must tell you it would be fascinating to watch what would happen if just once you took a different course and had to wing it on your own.'"

"He *didn't* say that!" Deline cried.

"Oh, yes, he did, and his remark stung. When he started to make love to me, I didn't want him to stop. More than anything in the world I wanted to know his possession. He was a virtual stranger, yet nothing about him seemed strange. Everything we did felt right. It was like I'd met my soul mate."

In a rare moment of pique Irena had risen to the bait and had done something foolish, if not dangerous, in order to prove he was wrong about her before she flew back to Athens. It had shocked her to the core, considering that from the moment he'd agreed to show her and the photographer around, she'd wanted to take him seriously, but was afraid.

Irena got to her feet. "After my new doctor's appointment this afternoon, I'm going to go back and tell Vincenzo he was right about everything. My being there will prove that I've taken a different course and want to be with him. We have this intense attraction and connection. It will be liberating to be able to admit it. If he meant what he said about getting married, I want it, too."

"What will you tell him about the baby?"

"The truth. As much as I've been told by the doctors. He has the right to know everything, including the fact that Andreas met someone else, too. If he can't forgive me for going back to break it off with Andreas, then he's not the man I thought he was." She bit her lip. "If he wasn't being serious about marriage, then I'll have to leave Europe."

"Where will you go?"

"I have no idea."

"Oh, Irena. I'm frightened for you."

"So am I. I'm terrified"

"Come on, Dino. You can do it."

"I'm scared, Papa."

Vincenzo could see the fright in his son's dark brown eyes. His medium-size six-year-old would only come as far as the edge of the hotel pool, but he wouldn't jump into his arms. No bribe would entice him. "Then what would you like to do before we leave?"

"I don't want to leave. I want to live here in Riomaggiore with you."

When Dino said it in that forlorn little tone, it gutted Vincenzo. "You know you can't, Dino. Come. We'll walk down to the beach and watch the boats."

"Okay," he demurred sadly.

"Would you like to go for a ride and catch some fish?"

"No. I just want to watch." Dino claimed he loved the water, but when it came right down to it, he couldn't bring himself to enjoy it. By now Vincenzo had hoped his son would have overcome some of his fears, but since his ex-wife, Mila, had remarried six months ago and moved to Milan from Florence, they seemed to have grown worse.

"Let's go!" He levered himself onto the tile. When both of them had slipped on their shirts and sandals, Vincenzo grasped Dino's hand and they descended the steps beyond the pool area that led down to the sea.

Tomorrow was the last day of his boy's one week summer vacation with him. Only a little more time left before he had to drive him back to Milan. Then the one weekend a month of visitation would begin again until his week in December. So much time apart from his son was killing him.

Before Mila had moved to Milan, Vincenzo

had made that once a month sojourn to Florence where she'd lived with her family and Dino since the divorce. He'd found a small hotel located near the Boboli Gardens where you could look out over Michelangelo's city. The delightful spot had become a second home to him and Dino.

The hotel he'd picked out in Milan didn't feel like home to them. Neither did Milan itself, but rules were rules and had been set in concrete. Vincenzo was only given one week in summer and one week in December before the Christmas holiday to be with his son on his terms.

Nothing would change until Dino turned eighteen, unless of course Vincenzo married again. Such an eventuality would upset a small universe of people in more ways than one.

But after letting his father dictate an ill-fated marriage the first time around, he was through with the institution. His only choice was to bide his time until Dino was old enough to plead for a change in the visitation rules. Then Vincenzo would go before a higher court and appeal the decision. Hopefully that day would come years before Dino was considered an adult.

Later, as they walked along the cliffside path of Via Dell'Amore between Riomaggiore and Vernazza, his son cried, "Look, Papa. The sun fell into the sea."

"Do you think it scares all the fish to see a big light shining under the water?"

That brought the first laugh of the evening to Dino's lips. "No. You're funny."

Vincenzo looked down at his boy. He was the joy of his life. "Are you tired after all our walking? Do you want me to carry you on my shoulders up these steep steps?"

"I don't think they're steep." He trudged up ahead of him, then turned around. "What's steep?"

Laughter poured out of Vincenzo. "Almost straight up and down."

"Sometimes I think I'm going to fall over."

"You keep going up first then. If you start to tumble, I'll be here to catch you."

"I won't fall. Watch!"

His strong legs dashed up the steps to the winding road that led to Vincenzo's apartment. Dino had straight brown-black hair and brown eyes like his mother's. His body type, like Vincenzo's, had been inherited from their Valsecchi line.

Of course Vincenzo thought his boy brilliant like himself, and good-looking like Vincenzo's mother. The Antonellos had a proud nose and firm jaw. All in all his Dino was perfect.

"I'll beat you to our house," he cried before hurrying up the last part of the road to the apartment jutting out from the cliff. From their balcony giving out on the Mediterranean, they'd spent many an hour looking through the telescope at swimmers and boats. When the sky was clear enough, they could pick out the constellations among the stars.

Dino ran around to the front door with Vincenzo not far behind. To his surprise he heard his son say, *"Buonasera, signorina."* They had a visitor. Walking around the purple bougainvillea, his heart skipped a beat because he'd spotted the one woman he never expected to see again. His thoughts reeled.

In the fading light her glistening black hair fell like a curtain from a center part to her shoulders covered in a sleeveless lavender top. Standing there on those gorgeous long legs half-hidden in the folds of her white skirt, the impact of Irena Liapis on his senses had never been more potent.

"Buonasera," she answered with a discernible Greek accent.

"Who are you?" Dino asked, but by then her startled eyes, dark as poppy throats, had come into contact with Vincenzo's. Since he knew she couldn't understand Dino's Italian, he took over, but he had to be careful what he told him. Everything would get back to the boy's mother.

"This is Irena Spiros from Greece, Dino," he explained. "She doesn't speak our language. That means we have to speak English to her."

"But I don't know many words."

"That's all right. Do the best you can with what you've learned. We'll find out how good your tutor has been."

"Okay." Dino turned and shook her hand. "Hello, Ms. Spiros. I am Dino and this is my papa."

She looked startled to hear her mother's maiden name used and Vincenzo could tell that she was also shocked to discover he had a son. But she recovered enough from both surprises to smile at him. "Hello, Dino. How are you?"

"I'm fine, thank you."

"How old are you?"

"I'm six. How old are you?"

She laughed softly. "I'm twenty-seven."

"Dino," Vincenzo whispered in Italian. "You should never ask a woman her age."

He bit his lip.

"It's all right," she said to Dino, having understood without translation. "You're a very smart, polite boy." Her eyes lifted to Vincenzo, a question in them, and he saw a glint of something undecipherable; anxiety maybe. He decided to enlighten her.

"When you came to Riomaggiore two months ago, my son was with his mother and stepfather in Milan. I've been divorced five years."

"I see." She studied him intently. "Dare I tell you he's adorable and that one day he'll grow up to be even more handsome than his secretive father?"

Something about her was different. He had yet to discover what it was. "You mean as secretive as the *almost* Signorina Simonides? According to the newspaper, she hasn't been available since the CEO himself sailed away with his new American bride."

He thought she might blush, or at least look away. Instead she said, *"Touché."*

Her lack of outrage was as surprising as it was intriguing.

Dino turned to him. "Papa? Can she come in?"

"Would you like that?"

"Yes. She's nice."

Agreed. "Then I'll ask her." He shot her a

glance. "He wants to know if you would like to come in."

She pondered the invitation for a moment. "Only if it doesn't interfere with your plans."

"Signorina Spiros wants to come in," he whispered to Dino, then moved forward to unlock the door.

Irena went inside but she feared her heart was pounding so loud, Vincenzo could hear it. After spending the last night of her business trip here two months ago, she knew his apartment fairly well. Comfortably furnished with a view of the sea to die for from the balcony, she found it incredibly charming. But something new had been added.

On the kitchen counter was an assembly of little boys' toys. The kitchen table had half a dozen board games sitting on top, one of matching cards still in progress. In the living room lay a soccer ball in one corner. A small golf club with plastic balls had been left in another corner. She saw a little bicycle propped against the outside railing near the telescope, all signs that a boy lived here.

Vincenzo had a son, but he'd never said a word about him. He came up behind her. His body was close enough she could feel his warmth. "Dino wants to show you his room."

She walked down the hallway to the door he'd opened for her. When she'd been here before, Vincenzo had indicated it was the guest bedroom, but he'd carried her past the closed door to his own room.

Inside she saw a lot more toys placed around, but what she noticed were framed pictures, some small ones on the bedside table and two large ones on the wall. They showed Dino and his father taken at different times and seasons.

Irena walked over to one of the photos where they were up on the turret of a castle in winter. Father and son were so attractive in their ski gear, she smiled. "I like this one."

"That is *Svizzera*."

"Switzerland?" she clarified. When he nodded she said, "Do you like castles?"

Vincenzo stood in the doorway. He translated for his son. "She wants to know if you like castles."

Dino looked up at her earnestly. "Yes."

"Do you have any soldiers? Or should I say knights?"

His son looked to him for help. After another translation Dino said, "I have um…forty."

"Forty?" she cried with a smile. "That's *molto!*"

When she spoke the Italian word, Dino laughed and rushed to a large case that he opened to show her all of his toy knights inside. She picked out one in full body armor and held it up to examine closely before putting it back. "This is an amazing army of warriors you have here." Vincenzo translated, causing Dino to beam. He was precious.

"Come in the living room," her host murmured. She moved past him and felt his gaze sweep over her. "Are you hungry? Thirsty?"

"Neither one, thank you. I ate at the Lido

Hotel before I came here. It's where I'm staying whilst I'm here."

"Did you come to Riomaggiore by train?"

"No. I flew to Genoa, then rented a car."

She moved through the apartment to the kitchen table. One of the games of jumping monkeys needed no translation; Irena wanted a little more time to gather her thoughts so she opened the box. When she smiled at Dino, he scrambled around the other side of the table to help set things up. He seemed eager to play.

After she took a seat, Vincenzo found his place at the end of the table and they started the game. For half an hour they scrambled to make the monkeys cling to the spinning trees. Dino taught her to say *scimmia* for *monkey*.

Irena really got into the game, causing Vincenzo to step up the competition. Dino let out a shriek of laughter, followed by Irena's. Things came down to every man for himself with Vincenzo's continual chuckle adding to the fun. Pretty soon all the monkeys lay on the table or had fallen on the floor.

As she helped put the game away, she checked her watch. She'd been here long enough. It was time for his boy to be in bed. So far Vincenzo had said nothing of a personal nature in front of Dino, but naturally he wouldn't. Irena knew absolutely nothing about the dynamics between him and his ex-wife, he hadn't even mentioned his marriage the last time she had been here. Doubt filled her that maybe she didn't know Vincenzo as well as she had imagined. What if she had totally misjudged their relationship? She walked around the table and put a hand on Dino's shoulder. "Thank you for letting me play. Now I have to go. *Buonanotte,* Dino."

In the next instant he ran over to his father, letting go with a volley of Italian. A conversation ensued before Vincenzo eyed her in amusement. "My son doesn't want you to leave. I told him we'd drive you down to your hotel."

"That's very kind, but not necessary."

"I'm afraid it is," he came back in an authoritative voice. "Now that it's dark, a woman who looks like you out alone on a summer night is a target for every male from fourteen to a hundred years of age."

Irena tried to repress a smile. "Only a hundred?"

His black brows quirked. "You'd be surprised."

Actually she wasn't. Young or old, the male of the species was the same in Greece, but perhaps not as unique or fascinating as the Italian standing in front of her.

It warmed her heart when Dino took hold of her hand and led her outside past the mass of flowers growing in profusion everywhere. The pale blue Fiat was practically invisible. Vincenzo had parked it right up against the rear of his apartment to make room for other cars, which she'd observed were rare in the village when she'd come here the first time.

While she stood by with Dino, his father started it up and pulled out on the pathlike road so they could get in. Dino hopped in the back and strapped himself in his junior seat. Vincenzo reached across the front to open the passenger door for her and then they were off.

He drove at normal speed, but the dangerous curves and twists of the steep road made it seem like they were moving too fast past houses painted in oranges, pinks and yellows.

"You're as nervous as you were before," he said in his deep voice. "Don't worry. I could maneuver this cliff with a blindfold on."

She believed him, but had to admit she was relieved when they reached the parking area of the hotel. Before she could move, his hand left the gearshift to cover hers. It sent heat up her arm. "I'm taking Dino back to his mother tomorrow. Come with us, then we'll talk."

"All the way to Milan?"

"It's not that far."

Irena didn't look at him. "Do you think that would be a good idea? You know what I mean."

"Are you worried about my ex-wife? Don't be. If taking you with me were a problem, I wouldn't have suggested it. You *did* come to see me, did you not?"

She couldn't deny it.

"Dino enjoys your company." He kept talking as if she'd responded.

"Your son is like every child. They're happy with anyone who pays attention to them."

"True, but you turned him into a friend when you took the time to see the things in his room and remark on the castle. That's his favorite picture. With you along for the ride, the trip will turn into an exciting adventure for him."

He squeezed her fingers a little tighter before letting go. "Do I need to add how much I've longed to be with you again? Two months have felt like an eternity. Naturally I don't expect it has felt that way to you. Otherwise you wouldn't have gone back to Greece, leaving me without any hope of ever seeing you again."

Vincenzo had no idea of the depth of her feelings. But when she'd discussed her plan with Deline, she hadn't known he had a son.

The very fact of Dino's existence altered the situation drastically.

Yet Vincenzo's words let her know nothing had changed for him personally. That tiny window of opportunity was still open for them to talk. If she didn't seize on his invitation, she might be sabotaging her only chance to salvage her life and that of the baby growing inside her.

The second doctor she'd gone to see hadn't been as convinced it was Andreas's baby. As he'd explained, pregnancy and conception were not hard and fast rules. It was just as likely to be Andreas as it was Vincenzo's and no one could actually tell her this for certain, especially since she'd only slept with Andreas twice! No doctor could be one hundred percent certain based on a few fleeting encounters. The agony weighed heavily with Irena, more so every day, and she knew that she had to talk to Vincenzo about the situation. If only she could be sure that baby was his!

"How soon do you want to get away to Milan?"

"We'll pick you up at nine."

Irena nodded. "How do you say *tomorrow* in Italian?"

When he told her, she looked over her shoulder. "*Domani,* Dino." She got out of the car and hurried toward the hotel.

CHAPTER TWO

IRENA LAY AWAKE FOR a good part of the night. Her demons wouldn't leave her alone.

Though she'd been a career woman since college, in the back of her mind she'd always imagined that one day she'd get married and have children. Somewhere along the way Andreas had become part of that fantasy.

Over the years their families had been good friends and had often remarked that the two of them possessed the qualities for the kind of match that would last. Irena had thought so, too, but once they had begun seeing each other seriously, Andreas had waited a long time before making love to her. Their intimacy had been satisfying but not explosive. This had caused her to lose some confidence.

She recognized early that he was a cautious

man. His reputation for not making mistakes put him, rather than his twin brother, Leon, at the head of the Simonides corporation once his father had to step down.

Though he'd assured her she was the only woman in his life, it hurt that he hadn't wanted to get engaged. He'd said he didn't believe in engagements. They'd know when the time was right to marry. She'd mistakenly assumed that the heavy responsibility placed on him as the CEO had dictated the amount of time they spent together.

If she were honest, she had to admit that between the hours he put in, combined with the travel she did for the newspaper, their relationship had suffered. When Vincenzo had pursued her so ardently, she'd been flattered and hungry for the attention.

But their ten days together and their one night of passion had turned into something more intense than a mere holiday fling. She knew then that her feelings for Vincenzo ran deep and now, seeing him again with his small son, those feelings were magnified. There was no question that Irena wanted this baby. She wanted it with all her heart and soul. And after witnessing Vincenzo's love for Dino, a part of Irena also longed for her baby to be Vincenzo's, too. But by the time she'd awakened at the hotel in Riomaggiore this morning, she'd changed her mind about following through with her agenda.

What she'd been planning since leaving the doctor's office was the act of a desperate woman. A *pregnant* one, she amended as she took the prenatal vitamins and antinausea pills he'd prescribed.

It was no use lying to herself. How could she think for one second that Vincenzo would feel the same way about her once she told him she was expecting a baby who might or might not be his child? He already had a darling six-year-old son of his own.

After brushing her teeth, she looked at herself in the mirror. Who did she think she was kidding?

What she needed to do was fly to someplace off the radar like Toronto, Canada. Her parents would understand she was trying to get over her heartache and wouldn't pressure her while she determined to make a new life for herself.

Toronto had a large Greek community. She could fit in using her mother's maiden name and have her baby. When it was a year old, she would go back to Athens, pretending to be a divorced woman. At that point she would be able to raise her child with no one the wiser and her secret forever safe.

Having made that decision, she dressed in white cotton pants and a silky, light blue blouse that tied at the side of her waist. The outfit would be comfortable to wear on the plane.

Before doing anything else, she wrote a note to Vincenzo explaining that it had been nice to see him and his little boy, but her plans had changed unexpectedly and she needed to make a flight.

Once she'd brushed her hair and slipped on her sandals, she was ready to check out of the hotel. It was only a short drive to the airport to return her rental car. If Vincenzo hadn't come to the hotel by then, she'd leave the note with the concierge.

At quarter to nine she arrived at the front desk and looked around. No sign of him. She paid the bill and left the note before walking out to the parking lot with her suitcase.

To her shock she discovered black-haired Vincenzo lounging against the driver's side of her car, causing a tumult of emotions inside her. How had he known which rental car was hers?

Tan cargo pants outlined powerful legs. In a claret-colored polo shirt with the kind of short sleeves that emphasized his hard-muscled arms, he could sell millions of magazines to any female who saw him on the cover.

He flashed her a stunning white smile. "Good morning, Irena."

"G-good morning," she stammered. "Where's Dino?"

"*Buongiorno!*" his son cried. When she

turned, she saw him hanging out the window of the Fiat parked in the next row. She'd been concentrating so hard on getting away, she hadn't noticed his smiling face. He wore a cute white shirt with a big green dragon on the front. "How are you this morning, *signorina?*" He had that question down pat.

"I'm fine, Dino. How are you?"

"Wonderful!"

Vincenzo had probably taught him that word this morning. He said it with such an endearing accent. Her gaze swerved to blue eyes studying her beneath a sun growing hotter by the minute. He stood straight and moved toward her.

"Follow us to Genoa so you can return your car before we head for Milan."

She took a quick breath. "Vincenzo— something's come up and I can't go with you after all. I left a note for you at the desk when I checked out… I have to leave, Vincenzo."

His jaw hardened. "I have no intention of reading your note, and you can't leave…not yet. You made Dino a promise to come with us. He wants to show you Rapallo's castle in the sea, built to repel pirates. He hasn't stopped speaking of it—you can't disappoint him."

One more look at Dino's expectant expression and Irena agreed. The only thing to do was drive to Milan with them. After Dino had been dropped off, she would ask Vincenzo to drive her to the Milan airport. She could leave for Canada from there.

"All right. A few more hours won't matter in the scheme of things." She reached for the key with the built-in remote and unlocked the door. He opened it and helped her inside, submitting her to another intimate appraisal before closing it. With an increased pulse rate, she started the car and waited to follow him.

During the short trip to Rapallo on the Italian Riviera, Dino turned in his junior seat and waved to her from time to time, making her smile. She waved back. When they reached the town, they parked in the historic center and ate gelato while they walked around the harbor.

She told Vincenzo to tell Dino that the tiny,

picturesque castle out in the water looked like
a toy castle. His son laughed and pulled her
hand as they walked across the short causeway
to explore it. Soon after, he begged her to ride
the cable car up to Montallegro. Who could say
no to him?

Along with other passengers they were treated
to a panoramic view of the Golfo del Tigullio.
After a lovely lunch at the restaurant on top,
they took the funicular back down to their cars
and drove on to Genoa where she returned hers
to the rental company.

Vincenzo put her suitcase in the trunk of the
Fiat where he'd stowed Dino's cases.

The sight of them and a bag of toys brought
a pang to her heart. In a little while the two of
them would have to part company.

Clearly Vincenzo adored his son. As for
Dino, he was crazy about his papa. How hard
for them to have to be separated, yet Dino had
a mother who must be missing him horribly.

More than ever Irena realized that in a few
short months she, too, could be faced with a

similar situation. If Andreas was the baby's father and he discovered the truth, then Irena would be forced to share visitation and the raising of her baby with him. But if Vincenzo turned out to be the father, then what would the future hold for them? Vincenzo already knew the pain of having to say goodbye to his child because of visitation; would he want to go through that again with this baby?

En route to Milan, Dino kept her entertained by teaching her a couple of simple children's songs in Italian. Vincenzo translated. She knew her accent was terrible, but she tried hard to memorize them and sing along. He corrected her here and there. By the time they reached the outskirts of the city, she could sing them without help.

"Bravo, *signorina*."

She shifted in her seat to smile at Dino. "*Grazie*. You're an excellent teacher."

He said something to his father in rapid Italian. Vincenzo answered back. Irena couldn't resist looking at him. "What did your son say?"

"He wishes you were his English tutor. Mr. Fallow was born in England, and moved here ten years ago. According to my son, he's strict and grumpy because of a sore hip. You're a much better teacher and you're very nice. He wants to know if you would you like him to teach you Italian."

Laughter escaped her lips. "I can't imagine loving anything more. How much does he charge?"

A smile lit up Vincenzo's blue eyes before he translated for his son. His boy giggled, then whispered something to his father.

Filled with curiosity she looked at him. "What was that all about?"

"He wouldn't say no to a chocolate bocci ball."

"Ah. A chocolate lover. I'll remember that, but what will his dentist say?"

This time Vincenzo chuckled hard. After he told Dino, all three of them were laughing, but it slowly faded as they were allowed through a security gate. Soon they pulled up in the courtyard of a luxury villa hidden from the road by foliage.

"I'll be right back." Vincenzo slid from the seat to get his son's bags.

Irena stayed in the car while Dino scrambled out of the back to come around to her door. She opened the window and shook his hand. "Thank you for a wonderful day, Dino."

"Thank you, too. You like Papa?" He looked worried. Of course he was wondering what was going on between her and his father. Did he want her to like his parent, or did he wish she'd go away and never come back? What would Dino make of a new baby brother or sister? A trickle of unease settled over Irena. Her baby could affect so many people's lives. She shook the feeling off and turned to Dino again.

"Yes, and I like you." She poked his stomach with her index finger.

He reacted with a grin. *"Ciao, signorina."*

"Ciao, Dino."

She watched the two of them carry all his stuff to the front door of the villa. A maid answered and let them inside. Assuming Vincenzo would be a while, she rested her head against the back of the seat and closed her eyes.

Though she knew what she was going to say to him when he came back out, she was full of trepidation. They hadn't been alone since she'd walked up to his apartment yesterday. Without Dino as a buffer, she didn't know what to expect from Vincenzo, and she had no idea how he was going to react to her news.

Vincenzo hunkered down in front of his son. "We had a good time, didn't we?"

"Yes. I loved it! Will Irena be with you the next time I see you?"

"I hope so."

"I do, too. She makes you happy, huh."

Vincenzo smiled at his son's insight. "Yes."

"Did you know she's afraid of the water, too? She told me while we were looking out of the castle window."

So…his son had an ally. "But she doesn't

seem to mind heights because she liked the cable car ride."

"I know. So did I. She's fun!"

"I agree."

Lowering his voice to a whisper Dino said, "She's beautiful, too, but don't tell *you know who* I said so."

"Don't worry. I won't. Now before *you know who* comes downstairs, give me a hug." He felt Dino's arms wrap around him and squeeze him hard. "I'll see you at the end of the month."

"I wish we could do stuff more often."

"But this is working, right?"

As Dino nodded and wiped his eyes, Mila appeared in shorts and a top, looking immaculate as always. His son broke away and ran toward her, giving her a big hug. She kissed his head before flicking her glance to Vincenzo.

"You're later than I expected."

In a gush of excitement, Dino told her all about their outing to Rapallo with Signorina Spiros. Vincenzo was perfectly happy for his son to take over and explain.

Mila's expression hardened. "Take your things upstairs, Dino. I want to talk to your father alone."

"Okay." He turned to Vincenzo. "I love you, Papa."

"I love you, too."

He grabbed his sack of toys and started up the steps. When he'd disappeared from sight, Mila turned to him. "You've never introduced Dino to another woman before. How important is she to you?"

"Very." Last evening he'd come close to cardiac arrest when he'd seen Irena at his front door. If he wasn't mistaken, Mila lost color.

"And she's Greek?"

"Dino's already said as much. Now I have to go, Mila. Irena is waiting for me."

"She's here?"

"*Sì*. She is in the courtyard in my car."

"How dare you bring her here, Vincenzo! And how dare you sleep with a woman in the apartment while Dino's there on visitation!"

"Save your anger, Mila. She stayed at a hotel."

"I forbid it, Vincenzo."

Vincenzo felt his own anger toward his ex-wife bubbling to the surface. "Forbid what? I've obeyed every edict of the visitation stipulation to the letter. There's nothing in it that states I can't be with a woman in my car or my own apartment in Dino's presence. My life has nothing to do with you anymore, Mila."

"We'll see about that!"

"If you and your father want to throw more money away talking to your attorney, I can't stop you, but I promise you'll be wasting your time."

"You won't be so smug when I tell your father and he gets the judge to alter the stipulation."

"That's not going to happen. *Ciao, Mila.*" With Irena's arrival, Vincenzo now held the trump card and he would use it.

"Don't you walk out on me yet!" Her strident voice had risen higher. "I'm not finished!"

"If you aren't, you should be. Dino has missed you. Don't keep him waiting."

He left the villa, knowing he'd put the handcuffs on Mila for now. It was always a wrench to walk away from his son, but for once someone was waiting for him. He found himself somewhat breathless as he got back in the car and turned to Irena. Elation filled him that they were finally alone.

The richness of her black hair held his gaze, but it hid part of her features. He leaned closer to smooth it behind her ear, unable to resist touching her before starting the car. He studied her beautiful Grecian profile for a prolonged moment before pulling beyond the gate and out onto the main road.

"I took this week off from work to be with Dino and don't have to report until tomorrow morning. Let's make the most of the time."

She stirred restlessly. "Vincenzo—I think we need to talk. You need to know the reason why I came…I didn't want to say anything in front of Dino."

"It's enough that you're here."

"I'm being serious."

"I never thought you weren't."

"Please listen to me. I won't be staying in Riomaggiore. I'm on my way to Toronto. If you'd be kind enough to drive me to the airport, I'll be grateful."

She was running away again. This time he wouldn't let her. "I thought you quit your job at the newspaper."

"I did."

"Then what's in Canada?"

"Another job away from Greece."

"If that's what you're looking for, I could offer you a public relations position at the plant in La Spezia."

He watched her hands clench together. "I don't speak Italian."

"I would teach you."

"Vincenzo—" she cried in frustration. "I stopped to visit you because I knew you would see the headlines about Andreas's marriage to

Gabi. It was important to me that you didn't think I was a total liar.

"When I left Riomaggiore, I went back to break it off with Andreas. After I met you, I knew that my relationship with Andreas was doomed—you were right about that. Andreas figured it out for himself, too."

Vincenzo was silent for a moment before speaking. "Be thankful Simonides acted on his instincts."

"Whether he did or didn't, I acted on mine and slept with you. That was the turning point for me." The attraction between them had been too powerful. They'd just gone with the moment.

He turned onto a road leading into a park. As soon as he could, he pulled to the side and shut off the engine before giving her his full attention. "Now tell me why you showed up at my door. The truth." Vincenzo was no one's fool.

"You're so sure I had an agenda?"

His penetrating blue eyes searched hers. "Let's just say you and I have a strong chemistry. Whatever the camouflage, I believe it brought you back."

He was right about the intensity of their physical longing for each other. "What if I told you the camouflage is hiding a compelling problem that has caused me to veer off course and fly alone?"

"I'm listening." He knew she was referring to the analogy about the geese.

Her heart thudded at the thought of her own daring. "Were you serious when you said you thought we should get married?"

"Perfectly."

She moaned. "That wasn't a fair question to ask you since the circumstances aren't the same as they were two months ago. I didn't know you already had a son and a troubled marital history."

"That's one way of putting it."

"I—I'm sorry your first marriage didn't work out—" her voice faltered "—but it's not just that. There is something else I need to tell you, something…"

"What is it, Irena? What is it that has changed since our last meeting?" Vincenzo was again silent for a moment, clearly in deep thought, before his gaze shifted to Irena once more. "Irena, are you pregnant...with my baby?"

Shocked at his insight, Irena lowered her head, hating what she had to tell him. "I'm pregnant, Vincenzo, but I don't know if the baby is yours. I've been to two OBs for opinions. Both worked out the timetable with me and came to the conclusion that we can't be sure either way who the father is."

"Simonides doesn't know?" Vincenzo was a proud man. She'd been expecting that question and was prepared for it.

"I only came from the second doctor yesterday afternoon before I flew here."

"And he's on his honeymoon..." Vincenzo's eyes narrowed on her face. "How soon do you plan to tell him?"

"I don't."

"As in never?"

"If you think that makes me an evil woman, I'll understand."

"Since I know you're not, why in heaven's name wouldn't you tell him? He has the right to know."

"It's a long, complicated story."

"I doubt it rivals my own." There he went again alluding to a life that she knew next to nothing about. "Go on."

"Look, Vincenzo. I've wasted enough of your time. I shouldn't have come here. Please just drive me to the airport."

"Not until you explain."

Irena threw her head back, causing her hair to resettle around her shoulders, and closed her eyes. Then she took a deep, cleansing breath before she began to speak. "It all started over a year ago when Leon, Andreas's brother, and Deline, Leon's wife, had a very serious quarrel. He was working long hours as Andreas's assistant, was hardly ever at home and it hurt Deline a lot. She accused Leon of neglecting their marriage and her. She wanted to start a family, but hadn't been able to get pregnant and things were bad between them.

"They separated for a couple months. When Deline told him she was thinking of making the separation permanent, Leon was so hurt he got his friends together and took out the Simonides yacht. His friends invited some women on board and everyone got drunk. Then a terrible thing happened."

For the next little while Irena relived the nightmare that had come close to destroying so many families. "I still don't know how Deline is handling it. Besides being pregnant with Leon's baby, she's taking care of the twins he fathered on board the yacht with Thea Turner that night."

"She must love him very much."

"She does. I believe their marriage has a good chance of making it. But if I were to tell Andreas about our baby, it could destroy not only him, but his marriage, too. Gabi's an innocent in all this and went through hell when her half sister died in childbirth. Until Gabi contacted Andreas, she was the one who took care of the twins for the first four months of their lives. If this baby is Andreas's, how would this news affect her?"

Vincenzo moved his hand to play with the ends of her hair. "The more the plot unravels, the more it sounds like my own complicated family saga." This was the second time she'd heard him mention anything about them.

"All the families have been in crisis, including mine. My parents had been counting on my marriage to Andreas. They've been grief stricken since he married Gabi. They think I'm heartbroken over it! If they knew it was his baby, they'd insist he take responsibility.

"And Andreas would insist on taking control, because that's the way he's made. But then everyone would get in on the act to make things right with me. Nothing would ever be the same again."

Hot tears rolled down her cheeks. "It would ruin so many lives—that's the reason why I have to keep this a secret from Andreas."

Vincenzo cocked his dark head. "Does anyone else know you're pregnant?"

"Does it matter?"

"Yes."

"Why?"

"If we're going to get married, I insist that everyone believe the baby is mine."

Irena gasped. "Vincenzo, what I said earlier... You don't want to marry me! Especially not now."

"Irena, the baby you carry has as much chance of being mine as Andreas's. As you have explained, he already has a wife, therefore I insist on taking responsibility. You need a husband, the baby needs a father and I need a wife."

"*Vincenzo...*"

"I'll ask you the question again. Does anyone else know you're pregnant besides me and your doctors?"

"Yes."

"Who is it?"

She bit her lip. "It's Deline."

Vincenzo rubbed the side of his jaw. "Under

the circumstances she's probably the only person you know who *could* be trusted. Do you think she'd be able to take our secret to the grave?"

Our secret. Irena couldn't fathom that he was really considering the idea of marriage to her, especially after what she had just told him.

"If I didn't believe that, I wouldn't have told her in the first place."

"Does she support you in keeping this from Andreas?"

"No. She's afraid that if I don't tell him, it'll come out one day anyway. But she would never betray me."

"Can you trust the doctors not to contact Simonides? He's too well-known for them not to make the connection."

"I did what you did when you told Dino my last name was Spiros. How did you know that by the way?"

"When you came before, I saw the name on your passport. Irena Spiros Liapis."

She blinked. "I'm surprised you would re-member."

"I've forgotten nothing about you, Irena." His velvety words melted through to her insides.

"When I went to the E.R., I told them my name was Irena Spiros. I was referred to the OB under the same name. Including the doctor I saw yesterday, none of them has any idea I was the other woman mentioned in the head-lines about Andreas."

"Then it's settled. We'll be married as soon as I can arrange it. Since you don't subscribe to any religion, we'll say our vows in a civil ceremony."

"Stop, Vincenzo!" She shook her head. "You're going way too fast for me…and yourself."

"Don't presume to tell me my own feelings, Irena. If it had been possible, I would have mar-ried you when you were here before."

She took a shaky breath. "Without my having met your son first?"

"I would have introduced you. The three of us

would have spent the day together before I asked him if he wanted to watch us get married."

Irena averted her eyes. "Whether he approved of me or not, he would have said yes because he loves you. He'll do anything to make you happy."

"But *I* wouldn't marry a woman unless she could make *him* happy, too."

"You hardly know me, Vincenzo. We hardly know each other."

"I know one of the most important things about you, Irena. You have an exceptionally kind nature that spoke to my son. After last night and today, Dino knows it, too. Shall I tell you what he whispered to me in the foyer before Mila appeared? He said he hoped you would be with me at the next visitation."

Her eyelids smarted. "He's very sweet."

"You took the time to play with him and make him feel like he was an important person."

"All children are important."

"Not everyone feels that way inside. I watched you with him last night. You put him at ease."

"I'm glad."

"Glad enough to marry me and help me raise my son while I father our baby?"

She avoided his gaze and stared out the side window. "It couldn't be that simple, Vincenzo."

"Of course not. I never suggested otherwise. We'll be one of those families of this generation that fits all the odd parts into one new whole. Hopefully it will work, but there are no guarantees."

Irena let out a sad laugh. "We're nothing alike."

His eyes grew hooded. "You and Andreas came from the same world, but you didn't make it to the altar. I wasn't as lucky as you, Irena, and didn't escape in time. My family thought I should marry someone like me, and you see what happened. I think being opposites with no expectations will be very good for us."

He'd said that before.

"I was in lust with you the second you walked in my office. That hasn't changed."

Her heart jumped. His honesty shocked her, but it was also that quality which had first attracted her. And his looks… She couldn't deny how physically appealing he was to her. Knowing he was already a father, having met his son, it surprised her that she found him more desirable than ever. But she couldn't allow that magnetism to blind her to the realities of the situation.

"I don't care what you say about Dino liking me. If we were to marry, he would feel another loss. You say you only get to see him one weekend a month and twice a year for a week. If we were to marry he would then have to share that precious time he has with you with me. The poor little darling would be so hurt."

In the next breath Vincenzo pulled her into his arms and buried his face in her hair. "Once we're married, everything will change for the better for both of us."

"Vincenzo—we can't even think about it without Dino having a part in the decision."

"I'm way ahead of you, so this is what we'll

do." He lifted his head, forcing her to look at him. "There's a hotel nearby where I always take Dino when I'm in Milan on visitation. I'll drive you there now and then I'll bring Dino back with me. We'll have an early dinner together and tell him our plans."

Everything was moving too fast. "That sounds good in theory, but you've only just dropped him back with his mother. What if she has arranged something special for him? He hasn't been home in a week."

A tiny nerve hammered at the edge of his mouth. She noticed it appeared when he was unusually tense. "If she has plans, it will be a first. As for my needs, this time they'll have to take precedence." After pressing a warm kiss to her lips, he let her go with reluctance and started the car.

CHAPTER THREE

BE THERE, ARTURO.

"Vincenzo! I saw your name on the caller ID and couldn't believe it. We haven't talked in ages. What can I do for you?"

"I need my attorney's help."

"Of course."

"I'm in Milan and am driving over to Mila's villa right now to pick up Dino. It's imperative I take him out for a few hours, then I'll return him. She's going to refuse because I only just brought him back from our holiday in Riomaggiore, but something's come up and it's vital I talk to him alone. Be the master counselor you are and call her attorney to let him know my special circumstances."

"I'll get on it right now."

"*Grazie,* Arturo." He clicked off.

Whether Arturo could reach Mila's attorney or not, Vincenzo had no intention of letting his ex-wife thwart him. She was already worked up because Dino had told her about Irena. He could just imagine the fireworks when he showed up at the door in a few minutes, but this was one time he didn't care, because hopefully it would be the last time he or Dino would ever be at her mercy in the same way.

"Signore?" The maid looked surprised to see him at the door.

"Would you tell Mila and Dino I'm here to see them."

"Sì."

He moved inside the foyer and shut the door. The noise resounded in the tomblike interior. Pretty soon he heard the patter of feet.

"Papa!" Dino came running into his arms.

Mila followed. "What are you doing back here?"

"Something important has come up. I need to talk to Dino for a little while. I hope you don't mind."

She had to think about it. "You can go in the salon."

"No, I meant I need to talk to him away from here, Mila."

"I don't want him leaving the house."

"Do you have plans for him?"

"We don't, do we, Mama?" Dino piped up.

"That's not the point, Dino."

"Then it won't matter if I take him for a few more hours. I'll have him back in time for bed."

"You've had your week with him, Vincenzo."

She didn't care that their son could hear this. Much as Vincenzo hated it, she'd left him no choice. "Legally I have the right to be with him until nine tonight. I bring him back early as a consideration to you, Mila. Go ahead and call your attorney. By the time you reach him, I'll have brought Dino back."

He glanced at his son. "We're going out to dinner."

"Can we get pizza?"

"If that's what you want."

"With *her?*" Mila demanded.

Vincenzo didn't answer. Dino walked out the door with him. It closed hard behind them.

"Mama's real mad."

"I'm sorry about that. She's missed you a lot."

They got in the car. "Are we going to eat with Signorina Spiros?"

"We are."

"Did she want me to come?"

"I'll say. In fact, she refused to eat with me unless you came."

A smile broke out on his face.

"Hey—our hotel!" he cried a few minutes later. "Is she waiting in our room?"

"Yes."

Irena thanked the clerk in the gift shop and took the two presents she'd bought back to the hotel room. Vincenzo had told her it was the one he and Dino always stayed in. They pretended it was their home away from home. The more she was getting to know him, the more she realized what an exceptional father he was.

If Vincenzo was the father of her unborn child, it would have no better parent. But she was getting ahead of herself. First they needed to broach the subject of marriage with Dino. These things took time.

Under the best of circumstances, his son might need months, even a year, to get used to the idea. Unfortunately Irena didn't have that long with a baby on the way. She still hadn't given up the idea of going to Canada.

Her ears picked up the rap on the door. Nervous over what was to come, she turned in time to see the two of them enter the room. It suddenly hit her they could be her future husband and stepson. As the thought penetrated, she was overcome by a myriad of emotions ranging from anxiety that it couldn't work, to excitement that it might.

"Hi, Dino!"

His brown eyes smiled. "Hi, *signorina!*"

Vincenzo's gaze traveled from one to the

other. "I've just told him we're going to have dinner here. I'll call the kitchen. He wants pizza. What else would you like?"

"Salad? Coffee?"

He nodded and picked up the house phone to place their order.

"Come over here, Dino." She'd put one of her gifts on the table. When he joined her, she told him to open it. Out of the bag came a canister of fifty pickup sticks. "Have you ever played this before?"

When he shook his head, she looked at Vincenzo. "What about you?"

A gleam entered his eyes. "Once long ago. We called it Shanghai."

"Well, the game I know works like this." She opened the top and put all the sticks in her hand. Then she placed it on the table and let the sticks fall. Picking out the black stick she said, "The trick is to remove each stick one at a time so the others don't move. The person who can remove the most sticks is the winner."

She got busy and loosened ten sticks before

disturbing some. Dino couldn't wait to be next. The game entertained all of them until their meal was wheeled in on a tea cart.

While they ate, Vincenzo took over in the translation department. "Dino? We brought you here to discuss something very important. It's about me and Irena."

"What is it?" Above his lips he had a milk moustache.

Irena exchanged a private glance with Vincenzo and they both smiled. "Do you know how you always ask me how come I'm not married and I always tell you it's because I haven't found the right woman yet?"

He nodded. "But now you've found Irena, huh."

When Vincenzo explained what Dino had said, Irena expelled the breath she'd been holding.

"Yes. We want to get married right away. How do you feel about that?"

Once the question was posed Dino said, "Can

I see you get married?" He'd asked it without hesitation. Vincenzo translated.

"We do everything together, don't we?"

Dino nodded. "Will Grandpa be there?" More translation.

"Not this time. Irena's family won't be there, either, because we're doing this too fast for everyone to get ready."

"It's not too fast for me!"

The look in Vincenzo's eyes as he translated said it all.

"Will Father Rinaldo marry you in the little church down the road?"

"I don't know. That's up to Irena." He explained what his son had asked.

Dino looked at her with entreaty. "It's a very pretty church," he said in English.

Irena didn't feel comfortable about that. Although she had strong feelings for Vincenzo, their marriage was going to be one of convenience first and foremost. Neither of them had expressed feelings of love for each other and they were really only marrying for the baby's sake. Vincenzo didn't even know if the baby was his or not!

"I tell you what, Dino. Your father and I will talk it over before we decide. Would that be okay with you?"

He let the subject go and asked another question before getting out of his chair to come and stand by Irena. He stared at her with an earnestness that melted her heart and asked her something in Italian. Again Vincenzo explained.

"He wants to know if you'll let him come to see us more often than once a month after we're married."

She didn't have to think about it. "Tell him I would love for him to come and live with us *all* the time, but I know he loves his mommy, too."

Vincenzo cleared his throat before enlightening his son. At that point Dino's spontaneous response was to reach out and hug her. Irena hugged him back, loving this precious boy already. Wiping the tears from her eyes, she told him to wait a minute. She got up from the chair and walked over to the phone table where she'd put his other gift.

"This is for you," she said in English, handing him the bag.

His face came alive in anticipation. "Two presents?" he said in the same language.

She understood what he meant. "Yes. Go ahead and open it."

He quickly pulled the little tied box out of the sack and undid it. Beneath the lid lay six chocolate bocci balls. *"Stupendo! Grazie, signorina."*

"Di niente, Dino." She'd heard that expression often enough. "Call me Irena."

Dino gave her another hug, then offered them both a chocolate. Irena declined hers, knowing how much he loved them, but his father had no reservations and popped one in his mouth. Dino followed suit.

"Delizioso," they both said at the same time. Just then she got an inkling of what Vincenzo would have been like when he was an

irrepressible boy Dino's age. The image would always stay with her.

They settled down to a couple more rounds of pickup sticks, then Vincenzo made the announcement that they had to go. "Your mama is expecting you, and Irena and I have to drive back to Riomaggiore this evening." To her relief, Dino didn't act upset they had to go.

"The game is yours, Dino." She put it in the sack and handed it to him. In his other hand he had his bag of chocolate and they left the room.

In a minute they were on their way to the villa. Irena was content to listen while the two of them kept up a rapid conversation in Italian. Dino had a dozen questions, firing one after the other.

It was like déjà vu when they drove up in the courtyard and Vincenzo told her he'd be right back. Except that this time Irena got out of the car to give Dino another hug and say goodbye. "*Arrivederci,* Dino." She was determined to learn Italian as fast as she could.

He grinned in delight. "*Arrivederci,* Irena."

The die was cast. Irena had committed herself. There was no going back. Vincenzo was forced to suppress his euphoria as Mila herself answered the door, ready to castigate him. But for once Dino didn't seem to notice the tension coming from her.

"Guess what, Mama? Irena gave me presents. She and Papa are getting married and I get to watch!"

"Why don't you go up for your bath?" Vincenzo suggested. "I need to talk to your mama."

"Okay."

"I'll call you tomorrow night and let you know everything that's happening, okay?"

"Okay. *Ciao,* Papa." He raced up the stairs with a new spring in his step.

Vincenzo eyed his ex-wife. Beneath her anger she looked anxious, and with good reason.

Since their divorce she'd had everything her way, but now that he was getting married, they could tear up the existing visitation agreement. "Thank you for letting me take him this evening. As you can see, it was important."

"I want to meet her."

"If you wish. Where's your husband?"

"Leo's in Rome."

"Shall I bring her in, or do you want to walk out to the car?"

Without answering him verbally, she moved past him and headed for the Fiat. Irena could see them coming and got out. She'd never looked more beautiful to him than right now standing there poised and elegant without being aware of it.

"Mila Ricci? May I present Irena Spiros from Athens," he said in English. "She doesn't speak Italian so we'll speak in English."

"How do you do," Irena said and shook Mila's hand. "You have a wonderful boy in Dino."

"Thank you," Mila answered in a brittle voice. She thrust Vincenzo an icy stare. In Italian she said, "How do you expect Dino to handle the situation when she can't even speak Italian?"

"She'll learn. Dino's anxious to teach her."

"I won't stand for it, Vincenzo."

He shrugged his shoulders. "You're going to have to."

"This won't change visitation."

She was in for a huge shock. Ignoring her warning he said, "You're being rude in front of my fiancée, Mila."

Her cheeks flared with color before she addressed Irena. "Do you have any experience with children?"

"No, but when Dino is with us, I'll try my hardest to make him happy."

Mila just found out Irena was a woman of high-class and breeding. It was impossible to fight good manners without looking like a shrew.

To Mila he said, "My attorney will be contacting yours. By Tuesday you'll know all my plans. *Ciao,* Mila."

Leaving her to digest that bit of news, he

helped Irena back into the car. By the time he'd walked around to the driver's seat, Mila had gone back into the villa.

"I feel sorry for her." Irena spoke once they'd reached the main road. "I don't think there's a mother alive who wouldn't feel threatened to know her child was going to be around the influence of another woman on a part-time basis."

He gripped the steering wheel tighter. "Perhaps now you have an inkling of how I felt when Mila remarried."

She nodded sadly. "Life shouldn't be this way."

"You mean everything should be perfect where every child gets to live with its own mother and father until he or she is happily married off and the whole wonderful process starts all over again?"

"Something like that," she whispered.

"You've already gotten a taste of what it's going to be like dealing with Mila. I'm glad she insisted on meeting you."

"So am I."

"In case her behavior has given you second thoughts, let me know now. I'll phone Dino to tell him there's been a change in plans. I don't want him to go to sleep tonight thinking that something's going to happen he's been wanting for such a long time."

"I don't understand. Why would your getting married make such a difference to him?"

"My story's as convoluted as yours. When I divorced Mila, I had to give up a lot to win my freedom from her. Dino was the main casualty, of course. He was so hurt by the tension in our impossible marriage, divorce was the only solution. But both our families disowned me over it."

"Are you joking?"

"I wish I were. If I wanted to see my child, I had to agree to abide by the severe stipulations she set up."

"Couldn't a judge have interceded?"

"Oh, he did, in favor of both our families. He and my grandfather were close friends, like your parents and the Simonides family. The order stated that Dino had been in jeopardy in a loveless home with a father who'd shown a flagrant disregard for his heritage and prominence, therefore was a poor role model."

"I don't believe it," she cried, aghast.

"There's more. Until the time came that I could show I'd come to my senses and had reconciled with my ex-wife, the visitation rules would stand."

"Oh, Vincenzo—that's horrible. None of those reasons make any sense."

"Of course not. Mila waited for me to go back to her, but she waited in vain. Finally she remarried six months ago, causing another change in Dino's life."

"Does he like his stepfather?"

"Not particularly. He's fifteen years older than Mila with a grown son and daughter at university. His wife died a year ago and it wasn't long after that he met Mila. He has nothing in common with a young boy like Dino."

"That must tear you apart."

"It does."

"So what will happen now?"

"Tomorrow morning I'll meet with my attorney to end the current visitation."

"What will you put in its place?"

"Joint physical custody. From now on Dino will have two homes."

"But the judge—"

Vincenzo shook his head. "Don't worry. After my attorney talks to Mila's attorney, everything's going to change in a big hurry."

"How can you be so sure?"

He sucked in his breath. "Because I'm prepared to do something I refused to do before. My father will be so overjoyed, he'll fall over backward to accommodate all my wishes, including that of influencing the judge to rescind his decision."

Irena had been listening between the lines. Whatever this something was Vincenzo had refused to do, it had to have been something big. So what was it the judge had meant about Vincenzo's heritage and prominence?

From the first moment she'd met him, she'd sensed he was a man of many parts. He knew too much, understood too much, had too much savvy to be an ordinary Italian male. There was an inherent authority and intelligence he emanated without conscious thought.

When they'd been introduced at the plant, she'd been aware of a certain deference the staff exhibited around him. Like he was someone elite.

She stared at his striking features as they sped along the strada toward Cinque Terre. Beneath his black brows, his aquiline profile gave him a fiercely handsome look. He had the most beautiful olive skin she'd ever seen. As for his eyes, they were so piercing a blue her body quickened just looking into them.

Irena felt like she was experiencing second sight. His sophistication couldn't be denied.

Who was this attractive man with unruly black hair who drove around in a secondhand car and rented a tiny apartment on a cliff? He dressed in casual clothes you could buy in any local shop and wore flip-flops like his son.

Without clothes he'd looked like a statue of a god she'd seen in Rapallo that morning. The memory of them making love six weeks ago sent a wave of heat through her body. Did she even know him at all?

"You're very quiet all of a sudden."

His low voice curled through her nervous system. "I've been putting the pieces of a puzzle together."

"How close are you to being finished?"

He knew she was on to him.

"Several are still missing. Just how prominent are you?"

"Let's save all that until tomorrow."

What was she getting herself into?

"Don't be alarmed. Once I've seen my attorney, I'll explain everything. Go to sleep. I can see your eyelids flickering. We still have an hour's drive ahead of us. After such an emotional day, you're tired and need to take care of yourself, especially now that you're carrying our baby."

Our baby.

The baby *had* to be theirs. It had to be! But still that dark cloud of doubt lingered.

Irena *was* tired. In fact, she was exhausted from too much thinking and feeling. "When should we tell Dino about the baby?" she asked after closing her eyes.

"Most likely he'll decide the moment. He's an incredibly insightful little boy."

She chuckled. "How long do you think it will take me to learn Italian?"

"Two months for the basics if you work on it every day. The rest will come over a lifetime."

"A lifetime. That's a beautiful thought."

It was the last thought she remembered until the next morning when she awoke in Dino's bed feeling slightly nauseous. She was still clothed except for her sandals. She'd completely passed out last night, forcing Vincenzo to carry her into the apartment after they'd arrived.

The shutters were still closed, but she could see the sun trying to get in. She threw off the light cover and staggered to the window to open them. A glorious view of the Mediterranean greeted her vision. She checked her watch. Ten forty-five. Irena couldn't believe it.

Vincenzo had placed her suitcase in the bedroom. She got out her cosmetic bag and padded to the bathroom.

She called out to him, but there was no response. He'd said he was going to see his attorney this morning.

She could tell he'd been in the bathroom recently. It smelled of the soap and shampoo he'd used in the shower. A wonderful male smell she associated only with him.

Once she'd swallowed her pills, she undressed and got in the shower. After she washed her hair with apricot shampoo, she dried it the best she could with a towel, then hurried back to the bedroom.

With a change of fresh underwear followed by a cotton top and pants, she felt a little better, but she needed something to eat. In the kitchen she discovered a note on the table from him, written with a flourish.

I should be back by noon and I'll take you to lunch. Feel free to nibble on anything that appeals. Crackers, toast might help with the morning sickness. There's tea or coffee in the cupboard, juice in the fridge. V.

She found a roll and grape juice. Perfect.

The food helped the emptiness in her stomach. She went back to the bedroom for her brush and worked on her hair until it fell in a swath. Since it was already warmer in the apartment than the other day, she arranged it in a loose knot on top of her head in the interest of staying cool.

Her pregnancy was causing her to notice everything. She'd thought her fatigue had been brought on by anxiety, but the doctor had assured her that it was normal to feel so tired, especially in the first few months.

Vincenzo already seemed to know and understand a lot more about her condition than she did. But then he had lived with his wife when she'd been expecting Dino. Irena had no doubts he'd taken amazing care of her.

She blinked back tears, not knowing the exact reason for being in such an emotional mood. Naturally it was a combination of everything, but she had to admit that part of it was the way Vincenzo had handled the situation. He was her rock.

Another part was her guilt. She needed to talk to someone about how she was feeling and reached for the phone to call Deline. Disappointed when she got her voice mail, she left the message for Deline to call her back. Then she phoned her mother, who answered on the second ring.

"Irena, my darling daughter. How are you? Where are you? Your father and I have been worried sick."

More guilt. She sank down on the side of Dino's bed. "I'm sorry. I meant to call you from the hotel in Riomaggiore, but the sightseeing trip with Signore Antonello took longer than I'd anticipated."

"You are with him again, in Italy?"

"Yes. You remember my writing about Cinque Terre in my article. It has those narrow, crooked streets lined with colorful old houses stacked haphazardly on top of each other. I think it's one of the most beautiful spots on the Mediterranean."

"You said that before. Is he a travel guide?"

"No, no. He works at Antonello Liquers in La Spezia. It's one of the places I highlighted in my article for tourists to tour. He was the man who took me around the village. Yesterday we went to a castle in Rapallo with his son."

"I'm glad if you're enjoying yourself a little bit. When I think what Andrea—"

"Don't go there, Mother. That part of my life is over. I don't want to talk about it again."

"I didn't mean to hurt you."

"I know. The fact is, Andreas and I weren't right for each other. I think we both knew it and tried to force something that wasn't there. Gabi's coming along proved it."

"What do you mean?"

"It's difficult to explain."

"But you *loved* him!"

It was hard to have a conversation like this long distance. "Yes, I loved Andreas. I always will." Frustrated, she got to her feet and began pacing right into Vincenzo who caught her by the upper arms to prevent her from falling.

By the enigmatic look in his eye, she couldn't tell what he was thinking, but there could be no question he'd heard that last admission. She eased away from him. "I have to go, but I promise I'll call you again tomorrow."

Irena hung up. "I—I was talking to my mother," she stammered.

"Have you told her about us?"

"Only in the sense that I knew you when I was doing the magazine article and since my arrival you've been showing me around. I don't plan to tell her anything else until our plans are formalized." She brushed her hands nervously against her hips, a gesture he followed with his eyes. "How did it go with your attorney?"

A heavy silence ensued. "Let's talk about it over a meal."

"Wait, Vincenzo—" He looked over his shoulder. "You came in before I finished making my point with Mother."

His face had become a mask of indifference. "You don't owe me an explanation of a private conversation with her. I walked in on *you*." On that note, he headed for the living room.

She followed him. "But I want to tell you."

He turned toward her with his hands on hips in a totally male stance. "Tell me what?"

"Mother's still living in denial about me and Andreas. If I'd finished that sentence I would have said, 'I always will love him as a friend, but I realize now that I was never *in* love with Andreas or he with me.'"

At the enigmatic expression on his arresting face, she added, "Otherwise I could never have gone to bed with you. No woman could do that if she were truly and deeply in love with another man."

"I agree," his voice rasped.

"Contrary to what you might think about me, in my twenty-seven years of life I've only been intimate with two men, and you're one of them."

His jaw tautened. "I never suggested you were promiscuous."

"No, but you'd have every right to think it after I fell like the proverbial ripe plum into your hands. I look back on it now and can't believe what I did. It still shocks me."

Miraculously, his compelling mouth broke into a half smile. "I confess I thought I'd died and gone to some heavenly place for a short while."

She'd thought the same thing, but couldn't bring herself to tell him that yet. "Vincenzo?" Irena eyed him frankly. "Can we put the past to rest? My relationship with Andreas? It's over."

He gave a slow nod. "Amen. Shall we go?"

Thankful they'd weathered that small storm she said, "I'm coming. Let me get my purse."

"How hungry are you?"

"I think a pasta salad would hit the spot."

"There's a trattoria across from the church Dino was talking about."

"I—I've been thinking about that," she stammered. "Maybe—"

"Irena—Dino assumed it would be a church wedding because that is what's real to him," he broke in quietly. "We don't have to do it there, and I understand your concerns about such an arrangement, but it will convince other people that our marriage is real. Wouldn't that be best for all of us, especially the baby?"

She knew Vincenzo was right and sensed he wanted a church wedding, too. Could she go through with such a public display for the sake of the baby growing inside her? She looked at the handsome man in front of her who was doing so much to help her. Smiling, she touched his arm tenderly before speaking.

"You're right. After we have a visit with the priest, we'll walk over to eat."

CHAPTER FOUR

VINCENZO GRASPED HER HAND. They walked down the road and around the curve, breathing in the fragrance from the masses of flowers blooming in pockets of explosive array. In ways she felt like she was moving through some fantastic dream.

Before long she spied a centuries-old yellow church on the right. He tightened his hand around hers. "Dino likes to go to church."

"He's so sweet. If our getting married here will help keep his world intact, then it's important to me. I'm thinking ahead to the baby's baptism, too."

A gleam of satisfaction entered Vincenzo's eyes before he opened the door and they stepped inside the somewhat musty vestibule. Beyond the inner doors she gazed around the semiornate interior. The lovely stained-glass windows gave the small church a jewel-like feel.

"Vincenzo?" A tall middle-aged priest had entered through a side door. The two men carried on a conversation in Italian.

Finally, Vincenzo said in English, "Father Rinaldo, this is my fiancée, Irena Spiros. We would like you to marry us."

"That is a great honor for me."

"The honor's mine, Father. I've brought the signed document giving you permission to waive the banns so we can be married in a private ceremony on Thursday."

His eyes smiled. "You are in a great hurry, then."

"You could say that," Vincenzo responded in his deep voice.

Heat rose from Irena's neck to her cheeks.

"It's about time, my son."

"I had to wait for the right one, Father."

"And how does Dino feel about it?"

"When we left him a short time ago, he said

he couldn't wait. Do you think you'll be able to fit us into your busy schedule?"

The priest's expression grew more serious. "For you, nothing is impossible."

Again Irena received the strong impression Vincenzo was someone of importance.

"Thank you, Father."

"Have you been baptized, Signorina Spiros?"

Irena nodded. "In Athens."

"*Bene*. Would one o'clock suit the two of you?"

Vincenzo glanced at Irena for her input. She nodded. "That will be the perfect time."

"Come ten minutes early to sign the documents."

"We'll be here, Father." The way Vincenzo was looking at her just then caused her legs to go weak. He cupped her elbow and ushered her out of the church. After the darker interior, the sunlight almost blinded her.

They walked across the street to the crowded trattoria. Tourists were lined up to get inside.

But she was with Vincenzo. When he appeared, suddenly they were welcomed on through and shown to a table on the terrace where the waiter hovered to grant them their every wish.

"You've made a conquest of him," Vincenzo murmured as the younger man hurried off with their order.

"You think?" she teased.

"I know. Have you forgotten I looked at you the same way when you swept into my office that day?"

Irena had to admit it had been an electrifying moment. At the time she'd tried to ignore what she was feeling, but apparently not hard enough as witnessed by the fact that she was seated next to Vincenzo and had just spoken to the priest who would be marrying them.

"Much as I like flattery as well as the next woman, I'm afraid the waiter's attention has everything to do with *you*. Who are you, Vincenzo? I'd like to know the man who's about to become my husband."

One of his brows quirked. "You know who

I am better than anyone. If you recall, I told you my family disowned me. But so it won't surprise you when we sign the marriage certificate, you should know my legal last name is Valsecchi."

She thought she'd heard it somewhere, but she couldn't quite place the name.

"Thank you for telling me."

He smiled the smile that had seduced her on her first trip here. *"Di niente*. I can't have my pregnant bride suffer from an attack of the vapors on our wedding day."

"I'm not the type."

"Grazie a dio." He drank the last of his coffee. "I think you've toyed with your salad long enough. Your cheeks look a little flushed from the heat. Let's get you back to the apartment. While you nap, I need to run over to the plant for a brief meeting with the staff."

A nap sounded good. He escorted her through the restaurant to the street. Once again they walked the short distance hand in hand, this time uphill. Vincenzo was a demonstrative, physical man who touched her often.

Irena discovered that with each contact, she felt more and more alive. When he saw her inside the apartment and told her he'd be back later, she suddenly didn't want him to leave.

After he'd gone she decided to lie down for a few minutes. It surprised her that when she heard her phone ring and reached for it, an hour had gone by. The pills the doctor had given her seemed to have kicked in. They'd taken her nausea away, but she found she was sleepier.

"Deline?"

"I just put the twins down for their afternoon nap so we could talk. Tell me what's happening."

Getting up from the bed, Irena walked through the apartment to the terrace laden with potted flowers of every color. She leaned against the railing, feasting her eyes on the breathtaking view. "There's so much to tell you I hardly know where to begin, but in a word, Vincenzo and I are being married on Thursday."

The palpable silence coming from the other end wasn't surprising. "You're really planning to go through with this?"

"Yes. I just came from meeting the local priest who'll be officiating."

"You're having a *church* wedding?"

"It's what Dino wants."

"Who's Dino?"

She bit so hard on her lower lip, it drew blood. "Vincenzo's adorable six-year-old son."

"What?"

"I know this is a lot to absorb. For me, too. Let me start from the beginning." For the next little while Irena told her everything.

"Oh, Irena...I don't envy you for having to deal with an ex-wife."

"I'm not thrilled about it myself."

"Yet you still want to go through this. Obviously you're crazy in love with this man, right?"

"Love? I don't know about that yet, Deline. I thought I loved Andreas. I know one thing—

he's bigger than life to me, Deline. Every minute we're together I find him more amazing."

"Maybe too amazing?"

She frowned. "What do you mean?"

"Have you asked yourself why he's willing to rush into marriage with you?"

"Deline—" she cried in exasperation. "I was the one who approached him, remember?"

"I know. I guess I don't know what I mean."

"He wants this baby and believes it's his."

"But it might not be his, Irena. If only you could find out before you go through with this marriage."

Irena sank down in one of the wrought-iron chairs. Her eyes closed tightly. "The last doctor I talked to said that only a DNA test could give me definitive proof of paternity."

"Then for all your sakes, I'd go get it done."

"I've been considering it."

"To tell you the truth, I'm surprised Vincenzo hasn't demanded it, especially as he is making such willing huge sacrifice as quickly as possible to keep you. He must be nuts about you!"

Irena jumped up from the chair. "I know exactly why he's marrying me, Deline. I figured it out the second I saw him with his son. That was no idle proposal he made two months ago. The fact is, he's bound to a strict visitation order. He wants his boy to be able to live with him and be with him as much as possible. For that to happen he needs a wife, but she has to be someone Dino can accept."

"Which means you've already won him over. There isn't a child in the world who wouldn't love you, Irena."

Tears pricked her eyelids. "You're a better friend than I deserve."

"Who helped *me* through the blackest period of my life?" she said almost angrily. "I'm glad if I can do anything for you."

"You already have by listening to me. In talking to you, I've come to a decision. No matter how painful it's going to be on everyone concerned, I'll never have a good night's sleep again until I know the truth about this baby's father."

Deline groaned. "Now you've got me worried."

"In truth it's all I have done since I found out about this baby, but for the first time my mind is clear. I know what I have to do. When I look back, I realize Gabi went to Andreas armed with the DNA results on the twins. Before he ever approached your husband, he immediately had them checked against Leon's DNA for a match. If I tell Andreas I'm having his baby, he'll want DNA proof, so that's the first thing that needs to be done."

All of sudden Irena heard Vincenzo calling to her. "Deline?" she whispered. "I have to go."

"Understood. Stay in touch."

This was the second time Vincenzo had walked in on Irena and found her on the phone acting furtive. She broke out in a smile. It didn't deceive him. "How did things go at your office?"

"Everything's been taken care of for the time we'll be away on our honeymoon."

Her smile cracked. "Vincenzo—"

"I was hoping some rest would have done you good, but you seem agitated. What's wrong?"

"There's something you need to know. We can't get married yet."

He was used to his gut taking hits, but this one penetrated. "If you're worried about a dress…"

She tossed her head back so hard, her hair came unfurled and the heavy weight swished against her shoulders. Much as he liked her gleaming black mane swept up, he preferred it undone. "You know I'm not."

Irena didn't have a vain bone in her fabulous body. "You said *yet*. What does that mean exactly?"

He could see her body trembling. "Once we're married I want to be a good stepmother to Dino, but first I need to consult another doctor and get a DNA test done. It's for all our sakes—" she cried as if he'd already protested. "I know I told you I wanted to keep it a secret from Andreas, but that was hysterical talk on my part. Of course he has to know the truth if the baby is his. I want answers as soon as possible."

Vincenzo thought he wanted to know right away, too, but already he'd been living in a fantasy where the baby was his. The pulse throbbed at his temples. "When did you decide this?"

Her eyes, those mirrors of the soul, glistened with unshed tears. "While I was talking to Deline. If I get a test done, it will remove all uncertainty. I'm afraid at this point I can't live without positive proof. Once I know the truth, we'll go from there."

As long as she wasn't refusing to marry him, Vincenzo could live with it, although he dreaded seeing the evidence that Simonides was the father. "Then we'll take care of it now."

She looked at him with pleading. "You don't hate me for this?"

"*Irena*—your pregnancy could be in jeopardy if you don't have peace of mind. Are you ready to go?"

"Yes."

They passed through the kitchen. She picked

up her purse and followed him out the door to his car. For once her thoughts were so heavy, she stared blindly out the window as they made their way down the dizzying cliff to the Via Colombo.

"We'll take the *litoranea* road to La Spezia. If you recall from the last time you were here, it's only a twenty-minute drive."

"The way *you* drive," she teased unexpectedly.

His lips twitched, relieved for the moment she didn't seem as tense. As she rested her head against the window, he turned on the AC and took advantage of the quiet to phone ahead to the hospital's E.R. Hopefully an OB would be available to cut down the wait.

Soon the traffic grew heavier. When they reached the sprawling city proper, he wound around to the hospital and parked. The lots were so crowded, Vincenzo was glad he'd called ahead to arrange for a consultation. After guiding her inside the E.R., they only had a ten-minute wait before an attendant called for Signorina Spiros.

They walked down a hall to a small office. The fortyish female OB greeted them in good English. "I'm Dr. Santi. What can I do for you?"

This was Irena's arena. Vincenzo remained silent while she launched in with her request. While she gave the background that prompted her to come in, the doctor sat back in her chair, eyeing the two of them with compassion.

"I understand how anxious you must be to solve your dilemma. However, that kind of procedure called Chorionic Villi Sampling can only be performed between ten and thirteen weeks."

"But that's another month away!"

"Yes. And there is some minimal risk."

Vincenzo reached for Irena's hand. "Explain, please."

"The test is invasive because cells have to be collected and this can cause certain risks for the fetus. Besides that, about one in two hundred women suffer a miscarriage because of this test. You need to weigh that against your need-to-know information. For example, you should consider whether not knowing the results will cause anxiety and whether knowing will be reassuring."

"We've already determined we *have* to know," Irena insisted.

Vincenzo had his own thoughts on the subject. Whether the baby was his or not he wasn't happy about her having the test. He couldn't wait to be a father again and didn't like the idea that this could hurt the baby in any way. Worse, Irena could lose it, putting her own life in jeopardy in the process. To lose her was anathema to him.

He stared at Dr. Santi. "Do you perform this test?"

"I'll oversee it. We have a perinatologist who does the actual procedure."

He glanced at Irena. "I think we need to talk about this more."

"Why, Vincenzo? Please understand."

Her agony was so palpable, he couldn't refuse her. "How soon does she need to come in?"

"Don't wait any longer than two weeks."

"I won't," Irena answered.

"If you'll check with the desk in Outpatient and set up an appointment, the next time you come in I'll examine you and get the blood work done."

"Thank you, Dr. Santi."

"My pleasure."

Vincenzo shook her hand and ushered Irena through the doors to the outpatient department. Near her ear he said, "Make it for two weeks. We won't be home from our honeymoon until then."

She stared at him in surprise. "Where are we going?"

"I'll tell you later."

He waited while she made her appointment, then walked her out to the car, knowing better than to try to talk to her until she'd had time for the doctor's explanation to sink in.

"Are you upset with me?"

Exasperated, Vincenzo pulled her into his arms. "I'm worried for you, for our baby, but I could never be upset with you. I can see you need this test so you can relax. Whoever the father is, it's you and the baby I care about."

"Thank you, Vincenzo." She hugged him back with surprising strength before getting into the car. On the way to Riomaggiore he stopped for petrol. He didn't need much, but used it as an excuse to buy them both a soda. She thanked him and nursed her drink all the way back to the apartment, clearly in an emotional state. Evening had fallen.

"Feel better?" he asked once they'd walked inside.

"No." Her voice wobbled. He caught her in his arms before she broke down sobbing. The need to comfort her was paramount in his mind. In a swift move he picked her up and carried her to the couch where he could sit and hold her.

"I don't want to lose my baby."

Cradling her in his arms, he kissed her cheek and hair. "No procedure's been done yet. Let's agree that for the next two weeks, we simply enjoy our honeymoon."

She'd buried her face in his neck, soaking the collar of his shirt. "What do you have planned?" Her lack of enthusiasm would have been daunting if he didn't know the reason for it.

"We'll fly to Los Angeles with Dino and do it all. A Hollywood film studio tour, Disneyland, LEGO Land, Sea World."

He felt her stir before she lifted her tear-ravaged face. "You're serious?"

Vincenzo nodded. "He's never been there. Have you?"

"I've been to New York many times, but not California. Since I started working for the newspaper I've focused my travel articles in Europe. What about you?"

"I promised Dino I'd never go to those places until we could see them together. Part of the visitation stipulation forbids me taking him out of Northern Italy. There was one time I broke the rules to go skiing with him in Switzerland.

Dino paid for it by not being able to see me for two months."

Irena threw her arms around his neck and hugged him. "How cruel."

She had no idea how cruel the powers working against him had been. He rubbed the back of her neck beneath her hair, needing this closeness like he needed water or light from a Mediterranean sun.

"If you haven't been able to spend more than a week with him at any given time, how can we be gone two weeks?"

"Being divorced tied my hands. On Thursday I'll be a married man and everything will change."

He heard a few sniffs before she sat up. "For both your sakes I'm glad things will be different. Looking back on my life, I loved my father so much that to imagine I couldn't have all the access to him I wanted while I growing up is incomprehensible to me." To Vincenzo's chagrin, she slid off his lap before he was ready to let her go. "I want to make this trip with Dino so enjoyable, he'll remember it all his life."

"The wedding day, too," Vincenzo murmured. "He needs a suit. Since I'll be tied up most of Wednesday with more legal matters, let's go shopping tomorrow. I rather like the idea of my fiancée picking out my wedding attire."

She flashed him a smile that came off mysterious whether she'd intended it or not. "You trust a Greek woman with a responsibility like that? Italian men are the best dressers in the world."

"I didn't know that."

"You can fool some of the people." When she laughed gently, it gave him a whole new reason to be alive.

"I need to eat something. Come with me and I'll make you my own version of bruschetta. Dino can't get enough of it."

"I'm afraid I'm hungry again, too. The anti-nausea medication is working. Now all I do is eat and sleep." She followed him to the kitchen.

"Unfortunately, every meal I've had in Italy has been divine."

Vincenzo chuckled. Her honesty was refreshing. When she liked something, she did it with her whole heart. While he got out the ingredients, she watched him. He liked that very much.

It didn't take long until he had their appetizers ready. "I'd offer you some of that local sweet dessert wine you tried the last time you were here, but it will have to wait until you've had the baby."

Their eyes fused for a moment. "The deprivation will be worth it."

He brushed her mouth with his own before he let her reach for a sample. The satisfaction of watching the food disappear pleased him no end. She stood at the counter next to him, munching away. Every so often she made a sound of pleasure.

Vincenzo loved that she didn't talk about how much weight she was going to gain. He liked every damn thing about her and needed another taste of her. This time when he claimed her lips, they were covered in extra virgin olive oil mixed with the tangy flavor of the herbs he'd added.

Divine didn't cover it, or the feel of her body as he pulled her against him. "I've been craving this all day. You could have no idea how much I want you." He kissed her long and hard. "The last two months were a desert after you left. Dino was the only reason I functioned. When are you going to admit you've missed me?"

"Isn't that what I'm doing?" Her muffled answer thrilled him.

"Irena—" Consumed with desire, he cradled her face, the better to kiss her features and eyelids, the passionate flare of her giving mouth. Back and forth they gave kiss for kiss, each one deeper and more prolonged.

They both heard the peremptory knock on the front door at the same time, effectively interrupting something private and marvelous. Irena's reaction was to pull away from him, but Vincenzo knew what the intrusion meant and clutched her to him possessively. The knocking grew louder.

She put her hands against his chest. "Someone isn't going away."

"News of our impending marriage has already leaked out through Mila's attorney." He kissed her palms one at a time. "One of my cousins has come to find out if it's really true. Probably Gino. Do you feel courageous enough to meet him if I let him in?"

"Should I be frightened?"

"He poses no threat, but *you* do by virtue of becoming my wife."

"Why?"

"Because I've been out of his hair for years, but after we get back from California he and my cousins are going to be seeing a lot more of me. I'll answer it before he breaks the whole place down. We'll offer him what's left of the bruschetta," he added, smiling.

But when he walked through the apartment and opened the door, it was his stepbrother Fabbio himself standing there. Apparently he hadn't trusted Gino or Luca to do his dirty work for him. Well, well... The whole nasty history between them flashed through his mind. Vincenzo could count on one hand the times he'd seen his flashy, dark blond stepbrother in the last seven years. *"Entrate, prego."*

"I prefer to stay where I am. Is it true?"

Some things never changed. Vincenzo looked over his shoulder. *"Innamorata?* Come and meet my stepbrother," he spoke in English.

Irena moved toward him. He knew he could count on her to remain calm in the face of surprise or an emotional storm, except when it came to the baby's paternity.

Vincenzo didn't miss the flash of stunned male interest in Fabbio's narrowed gray eyes when she joined them. After being thoroughly kissed in the kitchen, she'd never looked more desirable.

He put his arm around her shoulders, drawing her close. "Irena Spiros, meet Fabbio. Among his many talents, he's an *avvocato.*"

"That means an attorney, doesn't it?" With the

ease and unconscious dignity of a real lady she shook his hand. "How do you do, Fabbio."

Totally thrown, his stepbrother had trouble articulating. It had to be a rare moment when Fabbio, an inch taller than Vincenzo, was at a loss for words. "I've seen you before."

"People often say that to me. I must have the kind of looks shared by many women." Vincenzo had never met anyone who could think on her feet as fast as Irena.

"No." Fabbio wouldn't let it go.

She said something else to brush it off. "Won't you come in? Vincenzo just made us the most sensational food. If you don't finish the bruschetta, *I* will, and I've already eaten too much." With that voluptuous smile of hers, his married stepbrother's seduction was complete.

"Since I dropped in without invitation, another time perhaps." His eyes traveled from her glorious black hair down the curves of her body to her nylon-clad feet, presenting a picture of two lovers enjoying an intimate evening. He finally tore his gaze away to stare bullets at Vincenzo. Fabbio had wished him dead years ago. "If I could have a word with you."

Irena pressed his arm. "I'm sure you two have a lot to talk about so I'll disappear."

Before she could pull away, Vincenzo pressed a kiss to her red, slightly swollen lips. "I won't be long," he whispered.

She nodded. "It was nice meeting you, Fabbio."

Once she'd gone, Vincenzo lounged against the doorjamb, his hands in his pockets. "What's this about? As you can see, I have other matters pressing."

His cheeks went a ruddy color. "Mila just found out you're taking Dino out of the country for another two weeks on Thursday."

"That's right."

"The stipulation doesn't provide for changes."

"You know full well my marriage will have effectively done away with the rules of the divorce decree. The only reason you came here tonight was to see the evidence for yourself. Now that you've taken your full measure of my fiancée, I'd like you to leave."

His anger was near the surface. "You're not getting away with this without a fight."

"Surely that's for Papa to decide."

"He's ill."

"Only when it's convenient for him."

"Accidenti a te!"

"Curse me all you want, it will do you no good."

Now he was breathing hard. "The entire family stands against you."

"It was ever thus."

"You won't succeed."

"Careful, Fabbio. Your fear is showing."

"So is yours, or you wouldn't be doing everything in secret."

"Can you blame me for wanting to keep her away from the wolves for as long as possible? You're all waiting to tear her apart, but I won't have it. Irena is the most important thing in my life right now." He straightened and pulled his hands out of his pockets. *"Buonanotte, Fabbio."*

Irena appeared the moment he shut the door on him. "Don't you think it's time you told me about your family?"

He lifted one eyebrow. "Except for my mother who died seven years ago, I've been at war with them from birth."

She came closer, searching his eyes for the truth. "You're not joking." The pain in hers revealed she was devastated for him.

"Once upon a time I told you we were opposites. You come from a loving family and almost married into what I've gathered is a loving, forgiving family. I, too, love my father because he *is* my father, but I don't like him or my autocratic grandfather who's now deceased, or my stepbrother, or my uncles, not even my cousins once they started to resemble their fathers."

"Oh, dear."

"I sound like a monster," he ground out.

"No." After a moment of reflection she asked,

"Besides your mother, are there no girls in this fearsome group?"

With a sharp laugh, he let out the breath he'd been holding and grasped her shoulders. "Dozens."

"But they hold no sway in the male-dominated hierarchy," she divined with her rare capacity to discern the true nature of things. "How often is Dino around them?"

"Mila spends most of her time with them, so that means my son does, too. My father dotes on him."

"Who wouldn't? I'm crazy about him even after being around him such a short time. Does Dino share your feelings?"

"I'm not sure."

"How could that be? He tells you everything."

He shook his head. "Certain things he keeps to himself. In my case, I'm afraid my noninvolvement with family speaks for me."

"If he sometimes keeps quiet it's probably because he feels guilty."

Vincenzo kissed the end of her nose. "Why do you say that?"

"Because he knows how you feel and doesn't want to do anything that could upset or hurt you. *Or* get you in trouble," she added quietly before easing away from him. "From the sound of it, your intention to marry me has put flame to a fuse."

"You let me worry about that. The family has nothing to do with you and me. Our lives with our children will be our own."

She darted him a second glance. "I love Dino like my own child. Our *own* children... I want that more than anything in world."

Was Irena admitting she loved him because she'd accepted Dino? She still hadn't *our* baby yet. Vincenzo knew the doubt surrounding the paternity of the child weighed heavily on her shoulders. "I have a solution for us down the road, but only if you're willing."

"What's that?"

"One day we'll have another baby."

Her eyes suddenly filled. "Why do I get the

feeling you think that one woman in two hundred will be me?"

Vincenzo reached for her and held her close to his chest. "You're wrong, Irena. If you do go ahead with the test I'm sure everything will be fine and we will have a healthy baby. I just want you to know how eager I am to have a child with you. *Our child.* With no shadow of doubt hanging over us, and a child that will never have to leave this home. Our home. The truth is, I was never in love with Mila and she knew it. But both our fathers wanted the marriage and my ailing mother urged me to go ahead with it because she was convinced Mila would make me a good wife. She worried about my wild side."

A faint smile broke the corner of Irena's mouth. "So I didn't imagine you had one."

He bit her earlobe gently. "Mama feared I was enjoying my bachelorhood too much. Like all mothers and fathers, my parents felt marriage would have a stabilizing effect on me, so Mila and I married. It was the worst mistake of my life. To pay me back for not loving her, she didn't tell me she was pregnant until her sixth month when she couldn't hide it any longer."

Irena's expression revealed her horror.

"Dino came four weeks early. The two months before she delivered were the happiest I'd ever known because the idea of being a father had taken hold. But it turned into a nightmare after he was born. She refused to let me be around Dino and help with him. Her doctor called it postpartum depression.

"I recognized it for what it was. She couldn't hold on to me, but she wanted our baby to herself, nothing more. By the time Dino was three months old, I was completely shut out of his life. I told her we couldn't go on in our marriage that way. She told me there wasn't anything I could do about it. I told her I'd divorce her. She claimed I wouldn't dare."

Irena let out a groan.

"Hideous isn't it? When my father found out I was leaving her and realized he couldn't stop me, he disowned me, shouting that he never wanted to see me again. The only reason I was granted any visitation at all was due to my mother who prevailed on Papa before she died. To this day we haven't seen or talked to each other."

"So the wedding—"

"Will be a new beginning for my father and me," he broke in.

"How will our marriage change anything in his eyes?"

"I know my father. He never wanted to disown me, but he had to save face in front of Mila's father. Now that he's heard I'm getting married again, I'll go to him a new man and tell him I'd like us to start over. By reaching out to him, I'll have allowed him to retain his pride. He'll be overjoyed and speak to the judge who will give me back my full rights as a father."

A glint of suspicion entered her eyes. "A marriage to any woman could have helped you accomplish the same thing."

His spirits plunged. "Following your logic, I could have married years ago, but there's a flaw in your thinking. Why don't you sleep on it? Hopefully one day soon you'll have figured it out."

He drew in a ragged breath. "Go to bed, Irena. You look exhausted. I'll clean up the kitchen and see you in the morning."

CHAPTER FIVE

IRENA'S WEDDING DAY dawned, but she'd had a fitful night. It was a good thing Vincenzo had left early for the drive to Milan to pick up Dino. When she looked in the mirror and saw her drawn face, she was glad she had time to repair the damage before they returned.

Part of her restlessness stemmed from the fact that she hadn't told her parents anything since her last call to them. She vacillated whether to phone them now or after the honeymoon.

But as the morning wore on, she realized she couldn't put off telling them her news. To hurt them like that when they'd been such wonderful parents to her all her life would be unconscionable. She would have to tell them the truth. Not everything, but enough to satisfy them.

After getting ready for the big day, she

walked through to the kitchen to take her pills and make her phone call. As it turned out, her father had already left for work, so her mother phoned him there and they set up a three-way call.

"Irena? I've been anxious about you," her father began without preamble.

"I know. How are you?"

"Fine, but that's not the point." Her father sounded upset. "What's this about sightseeing with some Italian and his son? Who is he?"

She took a fortifying breath. "His name is Vincenzo Antonello. He's divorced and has a six-year-old boy named Dino. He manages the Antonello Liquers plant in La Spezia."

"The one you covered in the magazine section."

"Yes."

"Is he the reason you're still in Italy?" Her mother's question wasn't an idle one.

The blood hammered in her ears. "Yes."

"I'll never forgive Andreas for what he did to you," her father blurted emotionally.

"Please don't say that. I believe it was meant to be. He couldn't help how he felt when he met Gabi a-anymore than I could help my feelings for Vincenzo."

Her words were met with silence before her mother asked, "What feelings?"

Now was the moment. "When I met him two months ago, we spent all our time together. I didn't mean to, but it just happened. By the time I had to leave, he'd asked me to marry him."

"When you were already promised to Andreas?" Her father sounded stunned.

"I wasn't promised to him, Father. We weren't even engaged! It's true we both loved each other, but apparently not enough to make it to the altar. There were times he turned to Leon before he turned to me. I know now I was never in love with him. That's why I came back to Riomaggiore."

Her mother made a sound in her throat. "So what are you saying?"

She gripped the phone tighter. "Vincenzo and I are getting married in a few hours."

"A few hours—" both parents cried in unison.

"Yes. There's a church down the road from his apartment. A Father Rinaldo is going to marry us. I know this comes as a huge shock to you. To me, too, actually. You have no idea how much I love him. He's a wonderful man with a darling son." The realization that her feelings for Vincenzo had grown into love came as a shock to Irena, but the moment she said the words she knew them to be true.

Her father was the first to recover. "Does the boy live with him?"

Irena closed her eyes. "No. Dino lives with his mother. They've worked out visitation."

"So you're going to be a part-time mama before *you're* a mama!" Spoken like a mother.

Tears slid out from beneath Irena's eyelashes. "I'm very happy about it and hope you will be, too."

"When are we going to meet him?" her father wanted to know.

"We're taking a honeymoon to California for two weeks. I'll phone you when we get there.

After we return and everything settles down, the three of us will fly to Athens. Vincenzo's heard all about how wonderful you are and is anxious to—"

"Irena?"

It was Dino.

"I'm sorry, but I have to go. I promise to call you soon. Love you." She clicked off. "Here I am!"

Dino came running into the apartment wearing shorts and a dinosaur shirt. When he saw her in the dining room, he came to a full stop. "You are *bellissima!*"

It struck her how much she'd missed him. *"Grazie,"* she said with a smile before hugging him.

His brown eyes took in the cream-colored two-piece suit she'd bought in one of the boutiques. Around her neck she'd looped the matching colored lace mantilla she would put on when she entered the church.

While they'd been shopping she'd asked Vincenzo what he thought would look good in her hair. He'd said it didn't matter as long as she left it down.

"Is it time?"

She glanced at her watch. "Almost. I was afraid you wouldn't make it."

Vincenzo came in from outside, also dressed in shorts and a T-shirt. His eyes appraised her so intimately, she trembled. "After we left Milan, there was a terrible accident on the *strada* that held us up. Come in my room, Dino, and we'll both get ready."

"Your new suits are on the bed!"

"Fantastico!"

She could hear water running from the shower. Before long Dino came running back to the kitchen in his new navy blue suit and white shirt. Vincenzo had chosen the same outfit for himself. Both wore a blue-and-silver striped tie.

Irena reached inside the fridge and pulled out a florist's box that held two creamy baby roses and her corsage. She lifted Dino's from the tissue and pinned it to his lapel. When it was done, she kissed him on the check. "Now you look *bello* like your papa."

"Flattery will get you everywhere." Vincenzo spoke in his deep voice. She whirled around and met a pair of hot blue eyes. "Do I get a rose, too?"

He was incredibly handsome. Her mouth went too dry to talk. Instead, she reached for the other rose and walked over to him. Her fingers were all thumbs as she had to try several times to pin it on right. All the time she was fussing, Vincenzo placed little kisses here and there on her face, causing Dino no end of delight.

"Now it's your turn, Signorina Spiros." Near the shoulder of her suit jacket he fastened her corsage made of a cluster of cream-colored roses. "You do realize you won't be called that name much longer."

How could she possibly forget? Her impulsive trip back to Riomaggiore had come about half in a daze of pain and confusion, half with the ridiculous notion that Vincenzo might have meant what he'd said about the two of them marrying. Now here she was, ready to make promises to love, cherish and honor this man she'd only known for a short time.

Odd that she'd known Andreas for years, yet even after they'd started seeing each other as a couple, she'd never learned to know all the little things about him that she already knew about Vincenzo.

Every day with him, sometimes hourly, brought a new surprise. Part of the time she was breathless. The other part she found herself reeling with new information he fed her.

Feeling flushed and nervous, she turned to Dino. "I think we're ready."

"First some pictures." Vincenzo put his camera on the veranda table.

She caught his arm. "I just phoned my parents and told them we were getting married."

His eyes held a question. "Should I expect the police to descend on me before I can get you to the church?" he teased.

"No. They're not like that, but they'll want to see pictures."

"So will my father."

After he set the camera to take some timed shots, the three of them stood together in front of the climbing roses providing the background. After a dozen photos in quick succession, he said, "Let's go get married."

Dino led the way out of the apartment. They joined hands with him in the middle and made the same walk they'd done the other day beneath a hot, sun-filled sky. Tourists stopped them every few steps to congratulate them and take pictures. Her breath caught every time she looked at Vincenzo because he was so gorgeous. So was his little lookalike who wore a continual smile.

Soon locals had lined the road, clapping and cheering for them. To walk to the church for your own wedding surrounded by people who threw flowers petals at you was something Irena would never have imagined. But like everything else to do with Vincenzo in this dreamy garden paradise, it just felt right.

By the time they came in sight of the church,

the crowd had grown larger. At first she'd thought this was something that happened to every couple who said their vows here, but the deference paid to Vincenzo became too obvious to ignore.

She realized something else was going on. Irena would have asked him about it, but it was too late. He'd opened the doors and she had to let go of Dino's hand to arrange the mantilla over her head. Vincenzo helped her. "Have I told you yet how *squisita* you are?" he said in a husky voice.

He led her through the vestibule and down the aisle to the front where they sat on a pew. Soon a man and a woman entered from a side door. They nodded to Vincenzo before taking their places on either side of the aisle. In another minute Father Rinaldo appeared.

When he walked over, the three of them stood up. "You're late."

In a spate of Italian words Dino explained their delay.

The priest winked at him and patted him on

the head. "Accidents will happen. I understand."
He glanced at Vincenzo. "We'll do the paper-
work after the ceremony."

"*Grazie.*"

"Dino? Stand by your papa. Signorina Spiros
will stand at his other side. Vincenzo? If you'll
take Irena's hand, we'll begin."

She felt it curl around hers in a familiar hold
that warmed her heart. The priest performed
the ceremony in English. It was probably the
shortest church service ever given. No doubt
Vincenzo had everything to do with the choice
of language and the length.

They both made their responses at the ap-
propriate time and he eventually said, "I now
pronounce you, Vincenzo, and you, Irena, husband and wife. Amen."

He smiled at Dino and said something in
Italian. Irena saw her new stepson grin before
he answered, "*Sì,*" in a spirited voice.

Vincenzo turned to her. "Father Rinaldo just
asked Dino if he thought I should kiss my bride
now." On that note he lowered his mouth to

hers in a kiss sweeter than anything she'd ever known. Touched beyond words, she scarcely heard the priest say something else to Dino in Italian.

"Papa—" He tugged on his father's sleeve.

When she looked, he'd handed Vincenzo a gold ring. He turned back to her. "This was my mother's. She told me to keep it for the woman I would marry." So saying, he slid it on Irina's ring finger.

He really couldn't have loved Mila or he would have given it to her and it would have remained in her possession, but the whole circumstance of his first marriage was still a mystery to her. Vincenzo was his own man. She couldn't understand him marrying Mila because of pressure.

"Irena?" Her head jerked up. "Father Rinaldo has asked us to follow him to the vestibule so we can sign the marriage certificate."

"Of course."

Dino hurried ahead of them. The witnesses

signed first, then it was Irena's turn. She had to fill in Liapis after Spiros.

Vincenzo came last. She waited while he attached his signature. It took so long, she looked down at the paper. Her eyes widened in surprise because his name went on and on with a flourish.

Guilio Fortunato Coletti Vincenzo Antonello Gaspare Valsecchi.

After he'd signed it, the female witness gave Irena a slight curtsey. *"Congratulazioni, duchessa,"* she muttered.

Irena couldn't have heard the other woman right, but when she looked around to talk to her, she and the other man had slipped away.

"Vincenzo?" She caught at his arm. He lifted his dark head.

"Sì, Signora Valsecchi? I don't know about you, but I like the sound of it. Very much in fact." The smoldering look he gave her melted her bones.

"That woman just called me *Duchess*."

He had to sign another form. "Pay no

attention," he muttered. "It's a defunct title now and has been for years, but some will still insist on using it to feel important."

She refused to be put off. "You're a duke?"

"It's meaningless, *tesora*."

Irena turned to Dino. "Do you know who your father is?"

"*Sì*. He is Papa!"

"No— I mean— Oh—" she moaned in frustration. Vincenzo's low chuckle only added to it.

He finally stood up and handed the papers to Dino. "Will you run these inside to Father Rinaldo? We'll wait for you."

Dino nodded and dashed off. After he'd disappeared, Vincenzo pulled her into his arms. "All right. I'll tell you this once, and then we don't ever have to discuss it again. My father is the most recent Duke of La Spezia."

She blinked. "So the Valsecchis were once an important family."

"Once!" he emphasized. "At the time of my marriage to Mila, Papa was going through a cancer scare and had the title transferred to me. I couldn't have cared less about it. Unfortunately, the news made the papers. But then he recovered. After I divorced Mila he disowned me and the title was rescinded. That's all there is."

Irena shook her head. "That couldn't be all. Who was your mother?"

He studied her for a moment. "The Antonellos were a former royal family from the Ligurian region."

"And Mila?"

"Her family came from Florence and were of lesser importance. It means absolutely nothing, Irena."

"Except that in divorcing her, you were royally ostracized."

He gave an elegant shrug of his shoulders. "That's one way of putting it I suppose, but it's history now."

"Except that I'm a nobody."

"That's the beauty of it." His eyes blazed hotter. "I've finally gotten my heart's desire."

Before she could ask him what he meant

by that comment, Dino came running back. Vincenzo picked him up and gave him a hug. The two of them had a major conversation in Italian. Whatever his father told him, Dino ended up shouting for joy.

As they went out the doors of the church, Vincenzo translated for her. "I asked him if he was ready to go on our honeymoon. He said yes and wanted to know if it was a long, long way. I told him we needed to fly to get there."

"Has he been on a plane before?"

"No. When I told him we'd be taking the Valsecchi company jet in order to reach Disneyland, you heard his answer."

"Irena? Are you sad we have to go home today?" Dino looked so cute in his Indiana Jones hat. Vincenzo had gone down to the desk to take care of the bill, leaving the two of them alone for a minute.

"*Sì*, but I know your mama can't wait to see you. She'll love the presents you bought her." Throughout their trip they'd made arrangements for him to call Mila every late afternoon when she'd be up and available. Their conversations weren't long, but hearing his mother's voice every day probably cut down on any homesickness he might be feeling.

Irena couldn't believe that in the last two weeks she could actually understand some of his Italian and say a few phrases back, with lots of mistakes and plenty of laughs, of course. Still, they'd made a pact to speak it as much as possible and it was working. Vincenzo had told her she would learn Italian faster around his son than anyone else. It was true.

"Look!" she said to him. "We've had to buy two suitcases to hold all your new clothes and souvenirs!"

Her comment made him giggle as he ran around in his Indiana Jones costume. They'd bought him Indiana Jones LEGO to take home and build. Adventureland had been the biggest hit for him and they had gone there eight times, but he still couldn't find the courage to go on the jungle cruise.

Irena let him know she was nervous on boats, too, but would go on it if he would. She thought she was making progress when he got as far as the entrance to it, but then he had backed away.

Vincenzo kissed the side of her neck. "Thanks for trying to help him."

"Maybe I need to start with something simpler, like helping him get in a swimming pool. What if I took lessons with him? Do you think that would work?"

"Possibly. You have a special way about you."

"It's because I love him."

"He can feel it. That's why you almost talked him into it." *Almost* being the operative word. In the short time they'd been together, she felt like the three of them had become a little family. "Did I tell you you're going to be the most perfect mother? That little life inside you doesn't know how lucky he or she is."

She kissed the back of his hand. "He or she will adore you, too, Vincenzo."

They'd made the Disneyland Hotel their base. Dino had slept in his father's room containing two queen beds. Irena stayed in the adjoining room on another queen. Both she and Vincenzo had made that decision on the flight over. After their speedy wedding they felt it was important for Dino that she be eased into his father's life in increments.

In a few minutes, Vincenzo came back with a luggage cart and they left the hotel for the airport. Later on during the flight back to Italy, Vincenzo insisted she sleep in the bedroom while he and Dino bedded down on the fold-out bed in the club section.

It was Thursday when they landed in Milan. Two weeks had been but a minute. Irena found it difficult to let Dino go. Ahead of time they'd decided she would stay on board the jet. As soon as Vincenzo delivered him to his mother, he'd come back and they'd fly on to Genoa.

Vincenzo stood at the door of the plane. Irena walked Dino toward his father and hunkered down in front of him.

"We'll see you next Wednesday after school for your overnight with us." Vincenzo had worked out the new parenting arrangement: every Wednesday night, three weekends a month, eight weeks in summer, every holiday shared and nightly phone calls just before his son's bedtime.

Dino nodded. Tears filled those brown eyes, but he didn't let them fall. "I'll bring my new Indiana Jones game."

"Good. And this time I'm *not* going to fall in the snake pit."

He giggled, causing one tear to dribble down his cheek.

"I'll miss you, Dino," Irena said, "While we're apart I'll study my Italian and you can test me. Is that a deal?"

Vincenzo helped with that word because he didn't know it. "We have to go now, son."

"*Ciao*, Irena." He followed his father out the door and down the steps to the tarmac. The steward joined them with all his luggage.

Irena walked back to the club section. Before

she could even sit down, she dissolved into tears for Vincenzo and Dino, for Mila, for herself.

Years down the road she might have to face partings like this with her own child. Vincenzo had to do it all the time, already. How would he feel if the baby she carried was Andreas's? Would he feel the pull as much? Irena didn't know how he coped so well with the separation. He made a magnificent role model who was a superhero to his son. The baby just had to be Vincenzo's!

But whilst her heart hoped, another part of her tried to accept the possibility that it was Andreas's child she carried, because to think otherwise, the joy would be too much!

She wiped her eyes and pulled out her cell phone. It was time to stop dwelling on her own worries and ask Deline how she was doing. With both of them pregnant, they had a lot in common.

"At last!" her friend cried after picking up. "It's been a week since you called me. Are you still on your honeymoon?"

"We're at the tail end. I'm waiting in the plane for Vincenzo to take Dino back to his mother's house before we fly to Genoa." She could hear a lot of noise in the background. Children's voices laughing and screaming. "Where are you?"

"On Milos. Leon took the day off and we flew out here until tomorrow. All the families are in or around the pool."

"Then you can't really talk."

"Actually, this is the perfect time. Leon's causing most of the havoc."

"You've both needed a break. How are things between you?"

"Believe it or not, we're doing much better. Tell me about you and Vincenzo."

"We've had a wonderful time with Dino."

"Naturally, but I'm talking about the two of you, if you know what I mean."

Irena sucked in her breath. "We haven't had a real wedding night yet. I guess we already had it two months ago, but didn't realize it.

Right now it's important to make sure Dino's secure."

"You've taken on a stepson. That's a huge responsibility."

"True, but he's adorable. If I'd given birth to him, I don't think I could love him any more."

"I believe it." There was a silence. "And what about the baby you carry…have you thought any more about that? Andreas isn't back from his honeymoon. Leon thinks it will be another few days at least."

She lowered her head. "Tomorrow will be my first appointment with my new OB. She'll draw blood for some tests. The CVS test I'm having done won't take place for another two weeks.

"I've made up my mind that if it's Andreas's baby, I'll tell him the truth as soon as I have the DNA result in hand. I don't want to think about that scenario too much, but if it does happen I was hoping I could call on Leon to help. I thought he might know the best way to handle it. He and Andreas have such a bond. However if you think that's too much pressure..."

"Not at all. He's been where you are now. If anyone will have insight in how to break the news, it's my husband."

Irena almost broke the phone clutching it so tightly. "I'm so worried about Vincenzo, Deline. He doesn't talk about it a lot, but I have a feeling he is hoping this baby is his. I've never wanted anything so much in my life. But I'm trying to face reality now."

"I admire you for dealing with this situation as honestly and discreetly as you can. Now you're married to an exciting man who has taken you on, warts and all." Irena half laughed through the tears. "Is he still exciting?"

"You have no idea." However, there was so much Irena hadn't told her yet. Vincenzo had glossed over everything to do with his family background. Until she had a better understanding of why he'd dismissed his illustrious heritage and wouldn't talk about it, she couldn't discuss it with anyone, not even her best friend.

"Vincenzo's so good to me, I can't begin to tell you, but I'd better get off the phone now. He'll be back soon. I'll call you again before I have the test. Thank you for being the best friend on earth."

"The feeling's mutual."

CHAPTER SIX

VINCENZO BOARDED THE JET and told the captain they could take off now. He found Irena in the club section, sitting back in one of the seats with her eyes closed. Even after the long flight she still looked fresh in her two-piece yellow linen suit. She had marvelous dress sense and a glow about her from being in the Californian sun, but some of it could be attributed to the fact that she was pregnant.

He'd had two weeks to think about the possibility that the baby wasn't his. He still found it difficult to accept and knew he would find it hard to let the baby go to its biological parent, especially after Vincenzo had been forced to go through the same experience with Dino all these years. But at this point in time he was much more concerned for Irena's health and the baby's.

Sometimes when he allowed himself to believe the baby was his, the joy that filled him was almost too intense. He let out a ragged breath. Two weeks from now they'd know the truth and they would deal with it. Though she'd pretended everything was fine in front of Dino, Vincenzo sensed Irena's anxiety was growing more acute.

Unable to help himself, he walked over and kissed her exposed throat, one of her many delicious parts.

"Vincenzo—" Her eyes flew open in surprise.

"We're about to take off. Let me help you." He fastened the seat belt for her, then took the seat opposite her and strapped himself in.

"How did it go? Was Dino happy to be home?"

"I'm sure he was glad to see his mother, but Leo was there and it made things less natural for him."

"After these weeks of being together, I know

it will be hard on both of you to be apart. Thank goodness you only have to wait until Wednesday."

He gave her another prolonged kiss, loving Irena for loving his son, for understanding.

They'd already taxied out to the runway and were airborne. He waited until they'd attained cruising speed before undoing his seat belt. "Can I get you anything from the galley?"

"No, thank you. I had a soda while I was waiting for you."

He went in search of a cup of coffee. When he returned, she looked worried and gave him a searching glance. "How did Mila treat you?"

"Now that the tables have turned, she was unusually quiet."

Irena shook her head. "Surely she knows I could never replace her in Dino's eyes. She's his mother! If I can be his friend, that's all I'll ever be."

"There's more to it than that, Irena."

"What do you mean?"

"As long as Dino was our only child, Mila

never worried that he wouldn't inherit the title from my father one day."

"You said it was defunct," she reminded him.

"It is, but it's still of symbolic importance to her and her family. I could see it in her eyes tonight. She's almost apoplectic that there's the possibility you and I will have a baby in the future. That will mean Dino won't be the only one in line for the title and the money."

Irena left out a hysterical sound between a laugh and cry before eyeing him steadily. "Is it an extensive fortune?"

His lips tightened. "Yes."

"What does the Valsecchi family do?"

"Many things—investment banking, shipping, exports and manufacturing throughout eastern and western Europe. Now that my grandfather is deceased, my father, Guilio, is the CEO and oldest living member of the family."

"Is it a big family?"

"Average. The board consists of his two brothers, my uncle Carlo and my uncle Tullio.

Reporting to them are their five sons, my ex-wife's brother and my stepbrother whom you've already met. Each one of them holds the position of vice president for the various departments within the business."

"Where do *you* fit in?" she asked quietly.

"That's a long story. I was twenty-six when my mother died. You already know her feelings about wanting me married to Mila, so I became engaged, but I didn't set a date for our wedding because I needed more time. Except for a war separating you, I don't understand putting off marriage if you sense it's right in your gut."

He put his empty coffee mug on the side table. "Within six months my father remarried a widowed aristocrat from Genoa. She had a son, Fabbio, who was twenty-seven and a bachelor. He fell for Mila. If her ambition hadn't been so great, she would probably have been happy with him.

"Father saw what was happening. About that time he announced he'd been diagnosed with cancer. I believed he might have been making it up to manipulate me. I'm sorry to say it worked. I acceded to pressure and married Mila. After she became pregnant, father ended up in the hospital with prostate cancer. At that point I felt guilty that I had doubted him.

"He thought he was going to die and appointed me acting CEO. Up until then I'd been his assistant. At that point he transferred the title to me. Naturally these moves infuriated the rest of the family and the lawsuits started flying. It was brother against brother, cousin against cousin.

"To defuse the maelstrom, I refused the title. That not only upset my father, it infuriated Mila and her family. They treated me like a pariah. In time my father recovered, but wasn't speaking to me."

Irena made another sound in her throat. "How ghastly for you."

"With our baby on the way, I won't pretend it wasn't a hellish period. I was away on business for a lot of the time. By the time Dino was born, we were at war. As I told you earlier, she wouldn't let me have anything to do with him, so I divorced her. You know the rest. The cruel part began with the visitation order that pretty well stripped me of my rights."

She stared at him in a daze. "Where were you living until then?"

"In one of the smaller family palazzos over-looking the water in La Spezia. After the di-vorce, Mila continued to live there."

"And your father?"

"In the former ducal palazzo with his second wife where I was raised. It's higher up the hillside."

"I thought Mila went back to Florence?"

"She spent time in both places, but when it was my visitation, she managed to be in Florence. Anything to make it more difficult for me. These days she splits her time between Florence, La Spezia and Milan. Again, when it's my time to be with my son, I have to travel, but naturally I don't mind."

"How did you come to live in Riomaggiore?"

"The Valsecchi company owns several

hundred houses and apartments in Cinque Terre
that are rented out. I decided to take the one I'm
in because I favor it, and it's near the plant in
La Spezia where I work. Antonello's was part
of my mother's dowry when she married my
father."

The fasten seat belt light flashed on. They
were coming into Genoa.

"You're right," Irena murmured, fastening
hers. "Your family life has been much more
complicated than anything that has happened
to me." She smoothed the hair away from her
face. "Vincenzo? Why has marrying me allowed you to gain joint physical custody?"

He'd known that question was coming and
had hoped he could put off answering it for a
while longer. "I'll tell you when we're in the car.
From the looks of it, jet lag is already catching
up to you. Your beautiful eyes are doing that
little flutter thing." His comment caused color
to seep into her cheeks.

But Vincenzo knew that his wife, who still
had yet to sleep in his bed, deserved to know

what was happening. Their marriage might have been for convenience's sake, but he longed to make their marriage real. The truth was, he didn't dare make love to her until he'd cleared it with her doctor tomorrow. If being intimate could put the baby's life in any danger with the test looming, he would wait as long as it took. After all, he had the prize he wanted.

It was 10:30 p.m. by the time he'd ordered a limo to drive them to his car. Once he'd stowed the luggage and they'd headed for Riomaggiore, Irena had fallen asleep against the door. When he reached the apartment, instead of it being Dino he put to bed, it was his exhausted wife he carried to his son's room.

He removed her shoes and put a light quilt over her, relieved their talk would have to be postponed until tomorrow. Satisfied she wouldn't wake up, he went back to the car for their luggage and put as much away as he could.

After turning out the lights and locking up, he walked back to his bedroom and shut the door. Unfortunately he couldn't put off a certain phone call he'd promised to make as soon as he'd returned from his honeymoon. It was part of the bargain he'd struck with his father. With a sense of inevitability, he reached in his pocket for his cell and called him.

"So Vincenzo—you're home?"

"*Sì,* Papa."

"How's my little Dino?"

"After all his new adventures, he's thriving." He and Dino should have had a lot more like them over the years. Vincenzo struggled to tamp down his anger.

"Bring your wife to the palazzo tomorrow. Silviana and I have everything ready here for you to move in."

Bands constricted around Vincenzo's chest, making it difficult to breathe. "Tomorrow I'll bring her to the office. I'd rather your first meeting with her took place where I'll be working. I want to show her around, introduce her to everyone. Give us two weeks here at the apartment, then we'll make the move. Since we were married, I haven't had any time alone with her, Papa."

"You're that besotted?"

His father could have no idea. "I knew she was my soul mate the moment she was shown into my office and smiled." It got better from there. So much better that by the end of her business trip to Italy, they'd made love with a passion that still robbed him of breath. For those magical hours he knew in his gut she hadn't been thinking about Simonides.

"I guess I'm not surprised. I overheard Fabbio telling Tullio she was the most breathtaking woman he'd ever seen. That described your mother the first time I met her. How does Dino like her?"

Vincenzo cleared his throat. "I think very much, but you'll have to ask him if you want specifics."

"I intend to. Does your new bride want children?"

If a heart rate could quadruple, Vincenzo's did. With his next response, he would probably be struck by lightning. "To be honest, we've been so busy with Dino, there are many things we still need to explore. That's why we'd appreciate two more weeks without anyone else around."

"Then enjoy them while you can because you're going to be busy after that. I don't have to tell you how relieved I am you're going to be taking over, Vincenzo. As you found out when you looked over the books, we've had a downturn in profits over the last few years and we both know why."

"I agree the figures didn't look good."

"Your cousins simply don't have the grasp for business that you've always had. It's providential you came to your senses when you did. I'm tired of keeping it all together."

Vincenzo had come to his senses for the sake of his son and no other reason. His father wouldn't like all the changes he planned to make, but having been given two more weeks with Irena, he wasn't about to get into a detailed discussion tonight.

He thought ahead to tomorrow. Irena's doctor appointment had been made for midmorning. After they finished there, he'd take her to lunch at Spoleto's, one of his favorite spots. "We'll be at your office around one. *Ciao,* Papa."

"*Ciao, figlio mio.*"

His father hadn't called him *my son* in seven years. All that time he'd held Vincenzo hostage over a title! Rage welled in his heart. He swore an oath that he would never allow anything like this to happen to Dino.

Frustrated once more that she'd fallen asleep on him, Irena had awakened soon after Vincenzo had carried her in the apartment. She'd thought he would have taken her to his bedroom tonight. They hadn't been intimate for over two months. Now that they were married and alone, she didn't understand it.

Anxious to ask him what was wrong, she'd padded down the hall, but his door was closed. She'd heard him talking to someone, but had no idea who it was or what they were saying.

Feeling shut out emotionally as well as physically, she took a shower and got ready for bed. Her heart thudded as she left the bathroom, hoping he was there waiting for her. But the apartment was dark and quiet. Dino's bed remained empty.

A pain pierced her heart. When she'd first met Vincenzo, everything had happened so naturally, she hadn't had to think about which foot to put in front of the other. Now here she was his wife and she didn't dare tiptoe down to his room and climb into bed with him.

No one could have been more loving and attentive than he'd been in California. There'd been great tenderness, but they were home now. She needed reassurance that he still wanted her the way he had before.

After she climbed under the covers, she remembered something Deline had said several weeks earlier. *Have you asked yourself why he's willing to rush into marriage with you?*

Irena's response had been immediate. He'd needed a wife to change the rules of visitation.

Deep down she'd believed the attraction they had for each other portended something more significant. He'd said he'd gotten his heart's desire.

But if she was wrong and his desire for her was already fading, it was too late to do anything about it now because they were married. Dino was her stepson and trusted her. She had a baby coming. Although the paternity of the baby was still in question, Vincenzo had said he wanted to help her raise it.

Her parents knew they were married. While they were in California, Vincenzo had talked to them on the phone and he'd managed to charm them in his own inimitable way. Tomorrow she had her first medical examination with Dr. Santi. She'd gone past the proverbial point of no return. This was her life, the one she had made for herself. There was no going back.

This morning she took her time getting ready. Irena wanted to make herself look as beautiful as possible for her husband. She left her hair down the way he had said he liked it. After some deliberation she chose to wear a pale pink skirt with a shocking pink knit top. It had capped sleeves and a scooped neck. Combined with her tan and a new lipstick, she hoped she rated a second, even a third glance from Vincenzo.

He didn't disappoint her. She'd just finished her juice when he came in the kitchen and slid his arms around her. "You look good enough to eat." Irena turned around, anticipating a deep kiss, but it only lasted a moment. "You taste out of this world. If I nibble any more, we won't make it out the door to the doctor."

Another expectation dashed, but she hid her disappointment and reached for her purse. Following him out to the car, she could feast her eyes on his well-honed physique. Today he'd dressed in light tan chinos and a sport shirt in a brilliant blue that matched his eyes. Italian down to his hand-sown leather shoes, his dashing smile brought her senses alive.

As he escorted her into the outpatient department a half hour later, his potent male charisma drew the gaze of every female in the waiting room. It had been like that in California. He had admirers everywhere they went, yet he seemed oblivious to all the attention.

She had to concede he was more attractive than any film star or celebrity. It thrilled her that she was with him and could call this man her husband! Irena couldn't believe she was feeling and acting like a teenager when in reality she was a pregnant, twenty-seven-year-old woman.

"Spiros?"

Irena was so deep in thought, she didn't realize her name was being called until Vincenzo stood up. "That's you, *esposa mia.*"

She got to her feet and they walked back to a private examination room. After they sat down, Dr. Santi came in. She nodded to Irena. "You're looking well, *signorina.*"

"Actually, it's Signora Valsecchi now," Vincenzo corrected her. "We were married two weeks ago and just returned from our honeymoon."

"Ah...that explains the tan on both of you. Congratulations."

"Thank you," he answered for them.

"So, *signora,* have you decided you want to go through with the testing in two weeks? If so, we'll schedule it now."

"I made the decision the last time I was here. That hasn't changed."

The doctor switched her gaze to Vincenzo. "Are you in agreement, too? No second thoughts?"

"It's my wife's decision."

Vincenzo had said the words, but for some reason he didn't sound like he backed her. Perplexed, Irena turned her head to look at him. "I thought you were okay with it."

He covered her hand and squeezed it. "I am because it's what you want."

"But you still have reservations?"

The doctor stood up. "I'll leave you two alone for a minute to discuss it."

After she'd gone out, Vincenzo smoothed a lock of glistening hair behind her ear. "I told you before I'm not worried about you having a miscarriage, but I know that *you* are worried."

"Why do you say that?"

"Because you had nightmares on our trip— four of them, and another one last night. Something is bothering you."

Irena blinked in shock and covered her mouth with her hand, surprised and embarrassed by Vincenzo's insight. "How did you know that was what disturbed me?"

"You muttered the word *baby* each time. It shows how much you are thinking about this child you carry. I'm afraid you're the only one to determine if you can live with yourself if the test *does* cause you to miscarry. It appears you're going to have to weigh the possibility of suffering that guilt against your anxiety over waiting seven more months to know the outcome of the baby's paternity."

"They're all horrible choices."

He pulled her against him, molding his hand to the back of her head. "Irena, no matter what," he murmured against her temple, giving her kisses, "I'm here for you."

"I know that. I'm the luckiest woman on earth." She embraced him once more, then pulled away from him before she drenched his beautiful shirt. "Will you find Dr. Santi and tell her I want to go ahead with the test?"

"I'll be right back."

Vincenzo had scarcely stepped out in the hall when he saw the doctor walking toward him. "My wife has decided she wants to schedule the test."

"I think it's a wise decision considering her emotional state. I've a feeling the waiting will be harder on her. We want her to have as normal a pregnancy as possible."

He nodded. "Before you go in to her, I would like to talk to you about something. Since our marriage two weeks ago, I've been afraid to make love to her. Knowing there's even a minimal risk to the baby because of the test, I've hesitated to do anything that could add to it."

She gave him a frank smile. "You've just

saved me from telling you to hold off on the intimacy. Three more weeks with no problems and you can start to enjoy that side of your marriage.

"While I examine her, go to the outpatient center and have them direct you to the lab. I'll authorize them to do a swab of your cheek now. By the time the test is done and the results are in, you'll know if it's a match with your DNA. When your wife is through, she'll be waiting for you in the reception room."

"*Grazie.*"

He followed the doctor's directions and didn't have to wait long for his test. By the time Irena joined him in the lounge, he was still on the phone talking business with Bruno, his second-in-command at the plant. After hanging up, he walked her out to the car.

Before he helped her in he drew her close, looking down at the gauze taped to her arm. "Are you all right?"

"I'm fine."

"Are you hungry?"

"Starving." She said it a little too enthusiastically, but it meant she was making an effort even though she was nervous about the test. There was no one in the world like her.

"*Bene.* I'm taking us to a *ristorante* you're going to love." He kissed the lips he couldn't resist. Three more weeks… He didn't know how he was going to make it, but he had to for all their sakes.

Five minutes later they reached Spoleto's. The head waiter showed them through to the *terrazza* that gave out on a broader view of the Mediterranean. "Your usual table is waiting, Signore Valsecchi. Shall I bring the wine list?"

"Not today, Giovanni. We'd like iced tea and linguini for two."

When he nodded and walked off, Irena leaned forward. "What dish is that?"

"Linguini and their house sauce."

"That sounds delicious." She said the right words, but there was something else on her mind. "Before the waiter comes back, I'm waiting to hear the answer to the question I asked you last night. There's no royal line in my background, so how is it that your father has still been willing to get rid of the old visitation rules?"

"I've given him what he wants. Before we left on our honeymoon, I agreed to take back the title and be the cochairman of the company."

After a long period of quiet she said, "If you're not careful, you'll turn into my father. After he had to take over the newspaper business from his father, mother and I rarely saw him."

Irena's reaction was more than satisfying. It told him their time together was precious to her, too. He eyed her through veiled lashes. "But I won't let that happen to us, because I'm not like anyone else."

Her dark brows, perfectly shaped, knit together. "That's true, but a father and son running a conglomerate like yours will be consumed by business whether you mean for it to happen or not."

The waiter chose that moment to bring their

food to the table. Once he went away again and they'd started to eat Vincenzo said, "Father won't be cochairing anything. His cancer has come back. No one knows how much longer he's going to live."

"I'm sorry," she whispered, putting down the iced tea she'd been drinking.

"I am, too. One good thing about the title is that it gives me absolute authority to choose the person who will cochair with me. What I need is a young outsider with business savvy and fresh vision. The company has been losing business over the last five or six years."

"Because you left," she stated baldly. Her confidence in him reassured him as nothing else could.

"It's more a case of mismanagement and a bad economy. There are plenty of areas to attach blame. My way of doing things is to delegate once I've concluded the big contract negotiations. The detail work will be left to the others on the board who are capable of doing a good job if pointed in the right direction. Father didn't give them that much responsibility."

"That sounds good in theory."

"The changes I make will cut down on my workload. When I have to travel, you'll go with me and we'll turn those trips into vacations. Everything will be different."

"Are you thinking of asking Fabbio to help you? Being your stepbrother, he'd be a natural choice and is young like you."

Until Irena had come into his life, Vincenzo had felt like he was hurtling toward his old age at warp speed. Being with her was like finding the source of life all over again.

"There's no question Fabbio's an asset to the company. They all are in their own way, but after I chose to work at the plant, father did everything himself because he didn't trust anyone. No one has been taught to act or think outside the box. As a result, they're locked in a group mentality of business as usual. The company needs new blood for revitalization."

"It sounds like you've already made your pick."

"I have. It's a woman."

She looked down at her food. "In an all-male enclave?"

"Revolutionary, isn't it?"

"One of your dozens of female cousins?" Did he detect approval in her question?

"Not a cousin, but she *is* a relative."

At that revelation she lifted her head. Those dark, velvety-brown orbs had suddenly brightened. "Your father approves?"

"He doesn't know yet. When he does, it still won't matter. As I told you earlier, I hold the title now and can do as I please."

"I thought you hated it."

"This is the first time in my life I've had a change of heart about it. But I won't be keeping it for long."

She stopped eating. "Why?"

"When my father dies, I'll bypass Dino and bequeath it to my uncle Tullio while he's still alive. He's the next youngest Valsecchi brother.

Knowing him, he'll think he died and went to heaven. His first item of business will be to throw me out and crown himself CEO."

"Be serious."

"You think I'm not? You have no idea how much my uncles have envied my father. Tullio particularly has coveted his position."

She kept staring at him. "Then what will *you* do?"

"Go back as head of the plant and work around the people I like."

Irena made a sound of exasperation. "Sometimes I don't know when you're being serious or not."

"I guess you're going to have to take this on trust."

Her eyes moistened. "I do."

"*Bene.*" He put his napkin down. "How would you like to see Valsecchi headquarters?"

"Considering you're its head now, I guess I'd better. It would be embarrassing if someone asked me where my husband worked and I had no clue."

"It's only two miles from here in the marina district. Afterward I'm taking you sailing for the weekend."

A stillness enveloped her. He hoped it was because she liked the sound of it.

"I remember you telling me you had a sailboat when I was here the first time."

His eyes traveled over her features. "I wanted to take you out in it then, but it was in for repairs. It's a lucky thing."

"Why do you say that?"

"Because I might have sailed away with you and never come back. Once I met you, I couldn't keep things on a professional level with you."

"I'm afraid I couldn't, either, especially not that last night."

"Thank heaven for that. I was a thirty-four-year-old man you'd reduced to a besotted teenager who'd have done literally anything to get you to respond to me. I feared I didn't have what it took to entice the most beautiful woman I'd ever met in my life to stay with me another twenty-four hours."

Color seeped into her cheeks. "That last night with you was the result of a challenge you threw at me, one I couldn't *not* answer...." Her voice trailed.

One brow quirked. "For a woman as cautious as you, you showed a breathtaking response I suspected was in there somewhere, waiting to emerge."

"I had no idea I was that transparent."

"You weren't," he said in a serious tone. "It was wishful thinking on my part because I wanted you so badly and hated the thought of you ever leaving my bed."

"I didn't want to," she admitted, suddenly breathless at the memory of that night they had shared.

The chemistry between them was overpowering. Vincenzo reached over and held his wife's hand. "I'm longing to take you out on the water and show you some of my favorite places. There are isolated beaches where we'll relax and swim away from everyone else." He was counting the seconds until he could be alone with her.

CHAPTER SEVEN

IRENA'S HEART THUDDED to realize he didn't want their honeymoon to be over. Vincenzo intended to give her a true wedding night. Several of them in succession. She could scarcely breathe anticipating it.

Vincenzo fell silent as they neared La Spezia. Irena had found it perfectly charming before the way the city sprawled over the verdant mountains all the way down to the port. But this time as she looked up to take in churches and private estates clinging to the hillsides, she was aware that one of the more magnificent structures had to be Vincenzo's family palazzo.

The Valsecchi complex turned out to be a grouping of five buildings, each seven stories tall, surrounded by immaculately kept gardens. All of it was spread out over a large area.

Vincenzo parked in the VIP lot and escorted her inside the first building with the family crest emblazoned on the main doors.

He nodded to the security people and ushered her inside a private elevator. "This will take us to my suite on the seventh floor."

When they arrived, he walked her to a door where they entered a spacious, elegantly furnished office with a superb view of the sea. Oriental rugs covered the inlaid wood flooring. It resembled a drawing room with paintings, a coffee table, matching love seats, occasional chairs and a library of books.

Vincenzo walked around the large oak desk and buzzed someone on his intercom. On the wall behind him hung an enormous oil painting dominating the room. Inside its ornate gold frame stood the full-length representation of the duke of La Spazia in his royal refinery. He was probably in his fifties when it was painted.

"What do you think?" Vincenzo had slipped his arms around her waist from behind. "See a resemblance?"

"Maybe in his body type," she ventured, slightly breathless because she'd been craving this closeness since they'd left the doctor's office. Whether it was unconscious or not, his hand slid to her stomach and caressed her, as if he wanted to feel proof of the baby growing inside her. The intimacy of the moment caught her off guard and made her tremble.

He smoothed the hair away and planted kisses along the side of her neck. "I'm glad you didn't say his arrogance or swagger. Otherwise I would have been crushed."

"Well, now that you mention it…"

He spun her around so fast, her head reeled. His blue eyes smoldered with desire before he lowered his mouth, kissing her with almost primitive hunger. This was what she'd been craving. It matched her needs that had been growing since their honeymoon.

To go to bed alone night after night in that hotel room suite knowing Vincenzo was only a wall away had been beyond hard. But she'd wanted Dino to enjoy that special time with his father and not feel threatened by her.

Voluptuous warmth filled her body. She didn't know where one kiss ended and another one began. Irena was so far gone she didn't realize that anyone had come in until she heard a discreet coughing sound from the other side of the room.

Vincenzo slowly relinquished her mouth. With his gaze still fastened on her he said, "Come all the way in, Papa, and meet my wife. Irena Liapis Valsecchi. This is my father, Guilio."

The timing couldn't have been worse. She eased away from him and turned toward the door leading to the private elevator. Her first glimpse of his father gave her some idea of what Vincenzo would look like when he reached his seventies.

Guilio Valsecchi was a handsome man with streaks of silver in his thinning black hair. Their builds were very much the same, but the ravages of illness had taken their toll. He no longer had his son's vitality.

Vincenzo's father drew closer. His biting brown eyes scrutinized her. Like his son he could almost make you believe he could see through you. He might be suffering physically, yet neither age nor cancer had robbed him of that aura of authority inherent in his son.

He reached for her hand and kissed the back of it. "I've been anxious to meet the woman who brought about this miracle," he said in English.

"Miracle?" she inquired softly.

"I never thought the day would come when Vincenzo would change his mind and follow in my footsteps." His gaze flicked to the painting. "My ancestor had a healthy fear of powerful women." He eyed her again. "After talking with Dino about you, I can understand why. He believes you love him as if he were *your* little boy."

Irena swallowed hard. "He's very easy to love."

Guilio pursed his lips. "My daughter-in-law is having a difficult time."

Irena already knew that, but was surprised this would be the first thing he had to say to her, except that knowing Vincenzo even for such a short time, she shouldn't have been caught off guard. Her husband had shocked her with his frank speaking every step of the way since their first meeting.

"I don't blame her. There's a fine line between a mother wanting everyone to love her child and accepting the fact that there's another woman, unrelated, whose love for that child goes deeper than the surface."

Judging by the strange flicker coming from the depths of his eyes, he didn't know if he liked her answer or not. "What do you know about being a mother?"

The question assaulted her body, a body that was already carrying a child. Would she come to know this baby? Would the test be a success, or would she lose this precious baby growing inside her? The fear at such a loss almost overwhelmed her, but she fought to stay composed.

"Only what I learned from having a wonderful role model in my mother."

Vincenzo slid his arm around her shoulders and pulled her close. "Why don't you ask her about business, Papa? She grew up with an illustrious father who's one of the most revered businessmen in all Greece. Chief among his holdings is Athens's most prestigious newspaper. She grew up with it and worked in every department."

His father stared from one to the other without saying anything.

"Until two months ago she headed the coveted position of lifestyle editor, traveling all over eastern and western Europe. The photographer who came to Italy with her told me Irena has been her father's right hand for years."

Irena didn't know the two men had shared confidences about her.

"Rumor has it that when he's ready to step down, her father will name her to succeed him, but it's too late for that."

"How so?" his father finally spoke.

"Because I've made her my new cochair. She's going to help me run Valsecchi's. I've been single too long and do not want to be separated from my new wife now I have found her. Instead, we will work and travel together."

Irena almost dropped on the spot. She was surprised his father hadn't reached for a chair.

"I've brought Bruno over from the plant to be our assistant. This weekend he'll be setting up a desk and equipment for her in here."

Dr. Santi had cautioned Irena to take good care of herself and avoid any unnecessary upsets, but Vincenzo's bombshell had come close to blowing her away.

His father scowled at him. "You're not even going to throw Fabbio a crumb?"

"I have special plans that will challenge him and keep him busy. Since he seems to have a predilection for being enamored of the women in my life, I thought he would be better off in another building of the complex, separated from us."

The comment must have struck a chord with

his father because Guilio didn't argue with him. "What about Dino?" he asked in Italian.

"When he's living with us, we'll be home with him or taking him on trips with us, of course."

"But this is absurd. Your wife can't do anything when she doesn't even know the language."

Her husband had put her on the spot in front of his father, but right now she didn't want to appear totally lacking in front of his parent. "Your son and grandson have been teaching me," she interjected in passable Italian. "Dino makes a great tutor."

While his father shot her another look of incredulity, Vincenzo went on talking.

"Bruno is giving out memos to make sure everyone is assembled for the first board meeting Monday morning at nine. It's imperative the family meets Irena so we can begin laying down new policies. I'd like things to start turning around by our next fiscal quarter."

Guilio's expression hardened. "The others won't stand for it."

Her very Italian husband did that thing with his hands again. "Then they will have to look for another job—the way I had to do when you disowned me. It *could* be the making of them, but I'm not holding my breath. Now if you'll excuse us, Irena and I are still enjoying our honeymoon and have other things to occupy our time. *Ciao, Papa.*"

Irena had no choice but to follow Vincenzo's lead. *"A presto, signore."* She extended her hand, which he perforce had to shake. As her husband walked her out of the office to the private elevator, she felt his father's eyes boring into her retreating back.

On the way down, Vincenzo slipped his hand beneath her hair. He massaged her nape where the nerves were knotted from all the tension. "I can tell by your face you're not used to witnessing a relationship like I have with my father. Don't let it worry you. We understand each other."

"How ill is he?" she asked as he helped her into the car.

"That's difficult to say."

She bowed her head. "Your news set him back."

"Not as much as it astounded *you*, I'm afraid." Vincenzo flicked her an assessing glance after starting the engine. "But I know you and how much you love your work. Just because we're married doesn't mean you have to stop working. It will be fun running Valsecchi's together."

He was crazy, but it was a craziness that spoke to her soul. "What if the others revolt as your father said?"

"They won't. After what life has handed them, they don't have the kind of fire in the belly needed to break away and be self-starters."

Another fear grabbed hold of her. "You know the old adage about familiarity, Vincenzo."

"In our case it won't breed contempt. You need to understand something. I want you with me all the time."

In her heart of hearts she wanted it, too. When he'd first told her he was going to take over at

Valsecchi's, she felt like she'd been tossed into a void. She could see years and years of separation ahead of them caused by their business priorities.

"Later, when the baby comes, we'll deal with any changes." Vincenzo reached out and laid a hand on her stomach. "If the baby's not mine, I'm hoping you'll be able to work out joint physical custody to coincide with our time when Dino's at the house. He needs a sibling, even if it's on a part-time basis. They're both going to be young enough to bond."

She nodded, saddened to think of the turmoil ahead of them if this baby was Andreas's. "I would have loved a larger family."

"By the time my father gave me a stepbrother, Fabbio and I were too old to relate."

And your marriage deprived you of being a full-time father to Dino. The pained nuance in his tone haunted her. Waiting to learn if he was the father of her baby had to be the hardest test he'd ever had to endure.

* * *

Twilight had descended over the Golfo dei Poeti. According to Vincenzo, this was the place where Byron and Shelley, the British poets, used to come and actually lived for a time. Irena could understand why.

The medieval fishing village of Portovenere they'd just left sat like a little jewel in this part of Liguria. She'd eaten mouthwatering fish and Vincenzo's favorite pear-and-chocolate cake with hot chocolate sauce. When she couldn't manage another mouthful, he reached for her hand in a possessive hold and they walked along the promenade banked by the fascinating multicolored tower houses.

At the end of it they climbed the steps to the San Pietro church perched on a rocky outcropping. He pulled her back against his chest and wrapped his arms around her. With his chin buried in her hair, they had a superb view of Cinque Terre in one direction and the luxuriant green island of Palmaria in the other.

"That's our destination tonight," he whispered. "We'll anchor offshore until morning in a small sheltered bay away from people." Her body trembled with longing. She started back down to the port with him, eager to be away from the tourists milling about.

His gleaming white sailboat with thin black striping had a galley and one bedroom below deck. He handled the boat like it was a part of him. Having lived by the Mediterranean all his life, he'd grown up a water baby. When Dino had such a wonderful teacher in his father, it was strange he was still so frightened of it.

Irena wasn't that good at swimming herself. But Vincenzo loved everything to do with the water, so she was determined to learn, especially after he'd told his father he planned to vacation with her when they weren't at work.

"What does the *Spadino* mean?" The name had been painted on the side of his boat.

His white smile dazzled her. "Watch and learn." Once they'd moved past the buoys using the motor, the evening breeze picked up. He cut the engine and unfurled the white sail with a magnificent black sword imprinted on the canvas. It was so unexpected, she let out a cry. "Did you name it for a pirate, or because it cuts through the water like a sword?"

He sat at the rudder, guiding them toward Palmaria. "Neither reason, but I very well could have done and both would have made sense. The truth is, after Dino was born I bought the boat new and had the sail specially made to honor his name, which comes from Italian meaning 'little sword.' That's what a *spadino* is—a small or little sword."

"Oh, Vincenzo—how thrilling for him."

His smile faded. "You would have thought so, but he won't step on it. You saw how he was in Disneyland. He can't bring himself to go near the water."

"There has to be a reason." She walked over to him and put a hand on his shoulder. "Something has made him afraid."

He reached for it and kept it there while he kissed her fingers. "I don't know what it is. I fear he may have had an experience he won't tell anyone about, and the thought of him being afraid of anything saddens me."

Vincent didn't often show his brooding side, but when it came to his son she knew he couldn't help it. She turned to lean against the side as they drew closer to Palmaria.

He'd told her it was the first of three islands, the other two being Tino and Tinetto, charming names. As he angled them around the island she saw something unusual running down the steep hillside.

"What is that?"

"A slide where they once lowered black marble with gold veining from the quarry to the boats waiting where we are now." No ripple disturbed the surface here. "We'll sleep like babies tonight. If you want to go down and get ready for bed, I'll be there after I take care of the boat and lower the anchor."

"Don't you want some help?"

"I feel like waiting on you. It never leaves my mind for a second that you're carrying a baby." Tonight he didn't say *our* baby. Did Vincenzo fear that the baby might be Andreas's, too? Twelve more days before the test…

Irena left him and went below. She'd been hoping he would want to *help* her get ready for bed. On the night they'd made love—which felt like a century ago now—he couldn't help her out of her clothes fast enough. The sensual tension building for those ten days had exploded into a frenzy of need. Breathless, neither of them had held back.

But everything seemed different now that she was pregnant. Last night he'd taken them down the coast a little ways, telling her he'd join her shortly, but she'd waited so long for him, she'd fallen asleep. When she'd awakened, he was already up and dressed. He had breakfast laid out on deck for them.

He treated her like porcelain and at times with an aching tenderness that could make her cry. But the elemental fire burning between them before didn't seem to be there on his part anymore. If he hoped she would be asleep when he came down in a little while, he was in for a surprise.

The surprise ended up being on her. She waited an hour for him, but he never came down. Hurt beyond words, she put on her robe over her nightgown and went up on deck in her bare feet. She found him hunched forward on one of the banquettes, talking on the phone in Italian.

His conversation went on a long time. She couldn't imagine who it was on the other end at this time of night, unless there was bad news about Dino or his father. Nothing else could darken his handsome face with lines that made him appear older. She sat down on the same banquette to wait for him.

The second he felt her presence, he cut short his conversation and hung up. Because of the darkness, she couldn't read the emotion in his eyes, but she sensed he wasn't happy she hadn't fallen asleep by now.

"Who was that, or shouldn't I be asking?"

"You can ask me anything, but it was

Bruno, my eyes and ears, nothing important. Everything's fine."

Without preamble she said, "Vincenzo, after telling your father that you'd chosen me to be cochair of the company with you, I made the assumption that we would now share every-thing—our work, our thoughts, our dreams, our hopes, our fears, your son, the baby to come and…our bed. Please don't insult my intelli-gence and tell me everything's fine because I know it isn't."

Vincenzo stood up and rubbed the back of his neck, a sure sign he was contemplating his response and would have to choose his words carefully. That small gesture incensed her, prompting her to jump up. She placed her-self directly in front of him without touching him.

Her head flew back, causing her hair to swish against her shoulders. "Why don't you come out and say it—" she cried.

She heard his sharp intake of breath before

he clamped his hands on her shoulders. "What in the hell are you talking about, Irena?"

"You—me—*us!* I thought you'd brought me sailing so we could have our own private honeymoon."

"How could you have any doubt of it?" he asked in that silky voice guaranteed to render her witless with desire.

Fire turned her cheeks hot. "You're good at answering one question with another, Vincenzo. It's one of your best techniques when you want to evade an issue, but not this time!"

His hands flew up, palms facing her. "I swear I don't know what demon has gotten hold of you."

"I'm not a fool, Vincenzo." It thrilled her that for once her voice didn't tremble. "If you're suffering buyer's remorse for an impulsive moment you wish hadn't happened, just tell me! It can be fixed."

Lines bracketed his compelling mouth. "You're not making sense."

"Your marriage to me accomplished what

you really wanted. Now that you have the title, you're home free, Vincenzo. If you think your father won't celebrate to see the back of me, then *you* don't have the sense you were born with."

This time he gripped her upper arms and gave her a little shake. "Get to the point," he ground out. She'd never heard him sound so upset.

"Dino's not my biological son, so it won't impact his life if we get a quickie divorce. Contrary to what you believe, a career as co-chair of your company is not compensation for the husband I thought I was marrying."

He crushed her against him and kissed her so long and hard, she had no air left to breathe. "You know very well why I haven't touched you yet."

Through the layers of pain, the words resonated in her brain, leaving her reeling. She lifted her head, having to cling to him for support. "I have no idea what you're talking about…"

"Because of your pregnancy and the fact that the test is coming up! Dr. Santi told me that intimacy might hurt you or the baby at this early stage, especially with the test carrying so many risks for you both. She told me it would be better if we waited three weeks, until after the test, that way you'd be out of any danger."

Irena was silent for a moment, her features pale in the soft moonlight. She'd had no idea that her husband had been so thoughtful and suddenly Irena felt sick that she had reacted in such a selfish way. "I had no idea, Vincenzo…"

He groaned, pressing his forehead against hers. "I thought she would have talked about it with you, too. Obviously she didn't tell you the same thing."

"No," Irena murmured. "I wish she had— I've been so devastated, I haven't known what to do. It thought it was me…."

"Irena—" he said emotionally, "since we took Dino back to Milan, it's taken every bit of willpower I possess to stay away from you. If I had my way, we'd never leave the bedroom."

The relief of hearing the truth left her physically weak. "Then let's go down below and we'll just hold each other."

In the next breath he wrapped his arms around her, pulling her right up against him until there was no air between them. She felt his hands rove over her back with growing urgency. "I'm holding you right now and it's not enough." His breathing sounded ragged. "The way I feel about you, I can't lie with you and douse the fire you whip up in me. It isn't possible."

The longer their bodies melted into each other, the more she believed his trembling equaled hers. It was a revelation. She suddenly realized how completely she'd misjudged his behavior.

"Will you forgive me for the things I said?" she whispered against his lips.

"I'm glad you lashed out at me— It helps me keep sane until I can love you the way I really want to. Go to bed, Irena, before I lose my resolve."

In this fierce mood she didn't care to disturb

further. Her appearance had cut short his phone call with Bruno. Something was on his mind he had yet to divulge. But whatever else, Vincenzo still wanted her. For the time being she would hug that knowledge to herself.

"Where will you sleep?"

"Right here."

It was a beautiful night, warm and fragrant from the flowers growing in profusion on the island. She happened to glance down at the still water and saw something come up to the surface.

"Vincenzo? What's that? It must be almost two meters in diameter!"

His glance rested on the circular object. "It's the same moon fish that kept me company last night."

"Is it dead?"

"No. They sleep on the surface. I'll show you." He reached for an oar and dipped it in the water so it created a splash. The fish suddenly flashed its fin and descended below the surface.

"Oh, the poor thing."

He chuckled. "He'll find another spot in a few minutes and go to sleep again with nothing more to disturb his dreams than an irritating human. *Buonanotte, esposa mia.*"

On the way into the apartment the next evening, Irena heard her phone ring. It was the first call she'd had in two days. Not two hours ago Vincenzo had taken her to dinner at a delightful bistro in Vernazza, their last stop along the coast before coming home.

While he was bringing in their things from the car, she reached in her purse for the phone. "*Ciao,* Deline. *Come stai?*"

"It's scary how Italian you sound already."

She smiled. "That's because my husband is a wonderful teacher," she explained as he came in the living room. "It's Deline," she told him, knowing he was curious about her caller.

He pressed a kiss to her lips before carrying their bags on through.

"Call me when you can talk." Deline clicked off.

The abrupt cessation of conversation made her stomach clench in reaction.

Her friend had never done anything like that before. Vaguely alarmed, she tried to imagine what could be wrong. Of course, there could be a lot things. Deline could be having problems with Leon. Maybe she was having complications with her pregnancy. Yet Irena had the sinking feeling her phone call might have something to do with Andreas.

"That was quick." Vincenzo had come back in the room.

"She suddenly had to get off. I think a slight emergency with the twins. I'll call her back in a minute."

"In the meantime, do you want to talk to Dino with me? I'm going to phone him."

"I'd love it."

"Good. I'd like to pick him up in the helicopter, but he's never ridden in one before. I'll have to feel him out. If he's too frightened, then we'll take the plane to Milan and bring him back the same way."

She followed him over to the couch. After they both sat down, he punched in the digits. Before long Mila came on the line. In a brittle voice she said she'd put him on, but he couldn't talk long. A minute later they heard Dino's voice.

"Papa? Are you home?"

Vincenzo put him on speaker. "Yes. We just got back from a little trip on the sailboat."

"Is Irena with you?"

"Yes. She wants to say hello."

Irena had been practicing her Italian, hoping to surprise him. *"Ciao, amica. Come va? Mi sei mancato molto!"*

"Ehi—you have learned a lot!" he answered in Italian. "I miss you and Papa, too. Are you coming for me on Wednesday afternoon?"

"Sì," Vincenzo answered. "How would you like to fly in the company helicopter?"

"But there's no place to land!"

Vincenzo burst into rich laughter before

translating for her. Dino was adorable. "We'll land on the roof of my office."

"Is Irena scared?"

She thought she understood him. "No!" she called out.

On that note Vincenzo spoke to him a little longer, then ended the call. He pulled her onto his lap. "He said he'd do it because *you're* not afraid." His face sobered. "How have I lived this long without you?"

Her heart turned over. "Vincenzo—" She took the initiative and kissed the hard mouth she couldn't get enough of.

Irena hadn't meant to entice him. She wanted to keep her baby and had come to grips with the fact that they had to wait to make love until after the test. But she hadn't counted on the depth of her husband's passionate response or her susceptibility to his hunger that drove every kiss deeper and deeper.

Somehow they ended up on the floor with her half lying across him. This wasn't good. But it felt so good and so right, she couldn't stop what was happening.

"Irena," he said in a husky voice against her throat. "You're so beautiful it hurts. I want to kiss every part of you, but once I start, I won't be able to stop. We can't do this—"

He rolled her carefully to the floor, then got up to stand over her. His eyes burned with desire as he looked down at her. "I'm going out to cool off. I won't be long." In seconds he'd disappeared.

With her body still trembling from his touch, she got to her feet. Her hair was in total disarray. He couldn't seem to keep his hands out of it. As far as she was concerned, he could play with it forever.

When she saw her phone on the arm of the couch, she reached for it. Vincenzo's departure had given her the opportunity she needed to talk to Deline in private. She pressed the digits and walked out on the terrace where the heat of the day caused the air to hang heavy with the scent of jasmine and rose.

Irena was aware of an ache that brought warmth to the palms of her hands. Her pulse points throbbed in yearning to know his possession. That first time two months ago hadn't been enough. She knew it would never be enough.

A few weeks ago Vincenzo had admitted he was in lust for her. But what she felt for him was so much more than that.

She was a woman in love for the first time in her life. What she'd felt for Vincenzo paled in comparison to any other emotions of the past. She loved everything about the man she had married. If only she knew for certain that the baby she carried was his....

"Irena? Are you there? Can you hear me?"

Startled to hear Deline's voice, she cleared her throat. "Yes. I finally had a chance to call you back. You sounded so tense before you hung up."

"I take it you haven't seen a newspaper for a while."

She sank down on one of the chairs. "Go on."

"I think your father had an article printed to pay Andreas back."

"What do you mean?"

"I'll read it to you. The headline says, 'Only daughter of prominent Athens newspaper magnate marries titled CEO in Riomaggiore, Italy. After a whirlwind courtship, Irena Spiros Liapis, once rumored to become the future wife of CEO Andreas Simonides, has wed Vincenzo Antonello Valsecchi, Duke of La Spezia, in a private church ceremony.'"

Irena smoothed the hair off her face. "When I talked with my parents, I didn't know Vincenzo was titled, so how have they found out?"

"Your father's not a newspaper man for nothing."

"No." He might just as well have shoved a boulder down the mountain. Once the momentum picked up, there was no preventing it from flattening everything in its path till it reached the bottom. "Has Leon seen it?"

"He's the one who showed it to me. I thought I'd better call you."

"Is he suspicious?"

"Incredulous is more like it. I told him I knew you'd met a man when you'd been there on business for the newspaper and that when you went back, everything had moved fast."

Irena stared into space. "When Andreas gets home from his honeymoon, that's probably the first thing Leon will tell him, but frankly, I'm much more worried about Vincenzo's feelings. I love him so terribly, Deline."

"I know. That's why I hate to have to tell you that Andreas and Gabi are already back. They flew in this evening. Leon went to the airport to drive them home. I would have gone, but Nikos has a cold. At some point your marriage will come up in the discussion."

"It will."

"I'm glad you're having that test done, Irena. If Andreas puts two and two together and should call you, you'll be ready for him. Have you told your parents you're pregnant?"

"Not yet. Vincenzo and I have decided we'll fly to Athens with Dino and tell them in person after I've had the test. They always wanted to be grandparents. Deline? Thanks for this heads-up."

"Of course. We'll stay in close touch."

"Yes." Irena hung up and walked over to the railing.

That's where Vincenzo found her a few minutes later. She turned to him. "I'm glad you're back," she whispered emotionally.

He studied her with a questioning look in his eyes. "What did Deline say that has put that anguished look on your face?"

She told him everything. "I hadn't counted on my father being the one to inadvertently speed up the timetable."

Vincenzo stood there with his hands in his pockets, his expression solemn. "He loves his little girl and didn't like seeing her hurt. I can appreciate his reaction and the motivation behind his action. It was the most natural thing in the world for him to announce our marriage. He's a proud man."

"But he has no idea how the very existence of the title has caused you pain in your life. Now he has blurted it to everyone."

"You don't need to be concerned for me."

"But I am! I know how much you crave your privacy. I'm so sorry." Filled with pain, she hurried through the house to Dino's bedroom. She flung herself facedown on the bed, clutching the pillow like a life preserver.

In the next second, she felt the side of the bed give. Vincenzo leaned over her. "Forget everything, Irena. Relax." He rubbed her back "The only thing important now is you and the baby. We are going to have that test and then you are going to deliver a strong, healthy baby. I don't want you worrying about anything else."

CHAPTER EIGHT

IRENA HAD GOTTEN UP before Vincenzo. She'd prepared breakfast and had laid the table on the balcony. Along with a stunning linen suit in cream, the perfect foil for her dark hair and tan, she'd put on her serene countenance. You'd never know that within the hour she'd be walking into the conference room at headquarters to face a hostile environment.

During the drive into La Spezia, Vincenzo coached her on the opening remarks she planned to deliver in Italian. He felt an inordinate pride in her ability to be such a fast learner. Her accent wasn't bad, either.

Before long they arrived at the complex. Bruno, Vincenzo's auburn-haired confidant, stood at the entry to the conference room on the fourth floor. He'd met Irena when she'd come to Italy before. His smile grew broader as they exchanged greetings in Italian.

He flashed Vincenzo a silent message of approval. Vincenzo nodded before ushering Irena inside. The twelve, as Vincenzo thought of them, sat around the oval table in various attitudes of aggression, ready to pounce. Yet the moment they saw her, every jaw dropped. Fabbio's practically lay on the floor. Irena had the kind of looks that could stop weekend traffic on the autostrada.

He helped Irena to the seat next to his, but he remained standing. "Good morning, family. It's gratifying to know that during the years I've been away from the company, you've remained loyal to Papa. Before things go further, if any one of you, or all of you, wish to walk out now because you can't give me that same loyalty, I'll understand and we'll discuss your retirement privately."

As he'd predicted, none of them stirred.

"You've noticed several additions already. May I introduce my lovely wife, Irena Liapis, from Athens. I've asked her to be cochair of the company and she has accepted. We'll occupy the same office."

The pronouncement hit like a tidal wave, rocking them in their chairs. While they were digesting the news, he nodded to Bruno, who gave each of them a folder.

"Bruno Torelli worked with me at Antonello's. I've brought him here to be our personal assistant. He's an invaluable asset. If you'll take the time to read page one, you'll see the dossier on my wife's business credentials.

"She's a woman of many hidden talents. Her Italian is coming along beautifully, but it's not surprising. She speaks impeccable English. Because of her far-reaching family ties, she's also conversant in Serbo-Croatian and Slovenian. Those are areas where we do a great deal of business. I'm putting her in charge of them. She'll fit our needs like a hand in a glove."

While he heard coughs and quiet gasps, he glanced at his stepbrother, who so far hadn't been able to look him in the eye. "For years Papa has personally overseen the cottage industries, but now that he has stepped down, I'm giving Fabbio carte blanche."

Fabbio's gaze shot to his in astonishment. "You're eminently qualified for it and have been for a long time. Plan to set up your office in Building B with Gino and Luca."

He had two more assignments to make. "Uncle Tullio? With Papa gone, you will take over as company comptroller in Building C.

"Uncle Carlo? You'll take on Tullio's former area of responsibility along with your own and move to Building D." Tullio loved feeling important and Carlo disapproved of the way Tullio did business. These changes would satisfy both of them to some degree.

"All of you set up your new staffs and make the physical arrangements as you see fit." They needed their own space, something Vincenzo's father had never understood. "By Friday I'll expect reports on my desk. Irena will be taking the reports from Mario, Cesario and Valentino to get a grasp on the situation in the areas I mentioned. Now before this meeting is adjourned, she has a few words to say."

After his wife had delivered her small speech in perfectly adequate sounding Italian, he noticed a different feel steal over the room. She came across as a no-nonsense type, yet charming in her ultrafeminine way. They weren't happy with her, but they weren't feeling quite as mutinous as before.

Pleased that they all shook her hand before filing out, he liked the idea of working with his wife. As long as he kept her close to him, she would be forced to think about him. *Until the baby came.*

Last night he'd dreamed that the test results had shown Andreas to be the father. When she'd had to turn the baby over to Simonides for visitation, she'd fallen apart and Vincenzo hadn't been able to comfort her. He'd awakened in a cold sweat. He hoped with all his heart that the baby she carried was his child.

* * *

Irena eyed Dino across the kitchen table with her pocket dictionary in hand. Vincenzo had excused himself to take a phone call from Bruno. "Dino? Does your papa make you happy?" she asked in Italian.

"*Sì.*"

"Do you want to make him happy?"

"He *is* happy."

She smiled. "I know. He likes his boat. He wants *you* to like it." She'd been working hard to get her pronouns right and put them in the right place.

He looked down. "I like it."

"Let's go with him."

Dino shook his head.

"Why not?"

"I can't swim."

"Why not?" she asked again.

He answered with a word she didn't understand. When she looked it up, it meant *fear.* "You have *pauro?*"

This time he nodded.

She hurriedly searched for another word.

"You have fear of *pesce luna?*" The moon fish had startled her the other night, but she'd probably said it wrong.

"No." He bit his lip, then murmured, "*Squalo.*"

Once again she dug into her dictionary and found the word. She lifted her head. He was afraid of sharks! She understood. *"Capisco."*

Irena knew a great white had been sighted in the Mediterranean some time ago. It was a rare occurrence, but clearly Dino had heard something about the animals that had instilled a deep fear within him.

Later when they'd put him to bed, she discussed it with Vincenzo who lay with his head in her lap on the couch. He'd put on some music he'd thought she would like.

"I think I can see why he doesn't want to swim, Vincenzo. If he learns how, then in his mind he'll think you expect him to ride on a boat. It's a short leap from there to falling in the sea and being attacked by a shark!"

He reached up and pulled her head down.

"You've gotten something out of him I never could. My new cochair is brilliant." He kissed her mouth. "I've a feeling Papa told him something about the time he tangled with a shark when he was a teenager. It probably scared the daylights out of Dino."

Irena nodded. "I have an idea. When he comes on Friday for the weekend, why don't you ask him to swim with us in the Lido's pool because there aren't any sharks in there. Maybe it'll work and he'll slowly overcome his fear."

His eyes burned a flame blue. "I'll try it. Now I have another idea. Let's dance."

Yes!

The test was only nine more days away. If dancing was a way to get close to him for a little while, she'd take it. But the moment she stood up and melted into his arms, they clung to each other because he'd started devouring her with wild abandon.

Before she could say it, he told her it was time for her to go to bed in his bedroom. *Alone.* He would sleep on the couch as prearranged. What made any of it bearable was the fact that they went to the office together every day where she could feast her eyes on him and watch the genius at work.

On Friday Vincenzo's three cousins reported to her. She was still meeting with them when it was time to pick up Dino. She urged her husband to go without her. When the helicopter landed back at the complex, the three of them would drive home together.

Not long after he left, she was writing up her notes once the meeting had broken up when Bruno buzzed her from the reception room outside their office. "Are you free, Irena? There's a man here to see you."

She blinked because it meant it was someone not associated with the company. "Who is it?"

"He didn't say, but inferred it was urgent. Security has already searched him."

Irena had an idea who it was. Part of her had been expecting it. There was no one in the world more discreet than the man she'd thought she was going to marry. Andreas. That life and the woman she had been then seemed a century ago now. How much had changed!

"Please tell him to come in, Bruno."

"*Bene.*"

She got to her feet and waited. "Leon—" she said in surprise when Andreas's twin walked in the room wearing a tan business suit.

His gray eyes swept over her in alarm. "Sit down before you fall."

Irena didn't need to be prompted.

The man who would have been her brother-in-law rushed over to her chair with a glass of water he'd grabbed from a side table. "You've lost color. Here. Drink this. If you're not better in thirty seconds, I'm driving you to the nearest hospital."

"I'll be fine."

She drained the glass before looking at him. He was still hunkered down next to her. This close she could see the same expression he'd worn on his face for that month while Deline wouldn't have anything to do with him.

The time to speak gut to gut had come. "Does Andreas know about the baby?"

"No. He was sick when I picked them up at the airport. We called the doctor who thinks Andreas has picked up a bad bug on his honeymoon. He's in the hospital right now on an IV while he's being tested for everything under the sun."

"Andreas is ill?"

"I'm afraid so. His temperature's up and he can't keep food down." Irena heard the pain in his voice. Being Andreas's twin, she knew this had alarmed him.

"I can't believe it," she said in a quiet tone. "Poor Gabi. How is she?"

"Terrified for him, as you can imagine. She hasn't left his side."

"Of course not. Has he been ill long?"

"No. On the plane from Nassau he became so sick, his pilot and steward had to help him out to my car. When I eventually got home and told Deline, she broke down and it all came out about your pregnancy. She's panicked, we all are."

"In the beginning I was, too. But I'm not anymore, and she doesn't need to be." Irena put a hand on his arm. "Has he heard I'm married?"

"I don't know. He hasn't said anything." His breathing sounded labored. "Gabi's so terrified he isn't improving."

Irena could only imagine. If Vincenzo were lying in a hospital right now… "No matter what, you have to believe he's going to get better, Leon."

"One of the reasons I'm here is to make sure he doesn't get any worse. If he finds out about the baby…"

His words needed no translation.

"I can't stop people from talking, Leon, and I certainly can't prevent Andreas from jumping to conclusions."

"No. No one can do that."

"I have scheduled a test for a week from

Friday. By the time Andreas is better, we will know who the baby's father is. If it turns out to be Andreas, then I'll deal with it when the time comes. But until then, Leon, I'm assuming and hoping that this baby is Vincenzo's."

"You're a strong woman, Irena."

While he gave her a hug, she heard a young voice. "Irena?"

She pulled away in time to see Dino at the door. Vincenzo stood behind him, his features unsmiling. His eyes were veiled so she couldn't see any blue.

"Come over here, Dino." When she motioned to him, he ran to her so they could hug. "Dino, I'd like you to meet Leon. He's the husband of my best friend, Deline. I told you about her." The boy nodded.

Darting Leon a glance she said, "Leonides Simonides, this is my *stupendo* stepson, Dino." The way she'd worded it made him giggle.

Leon smiled. *"Ciao, Dino. Come stai?"*

She'd forgotten their family could converse in basic Italian. Her heart thudded as Vincenzo moved toward them. "Leon, this is my husband, Vincenzo Valsecchi."

The two men shook hands. "Congratulations on your marriage, Signore Valsecchi. Irena and her family have been friends of our family for many years. I've always said the person who won her heart would be the luckiest of men."

"*Grazie,* Signore Simonides." Her husband gave a polite response. "What brings you all this way?"

Her heart was jumping in her throat. "Andreas came home ill from his honeymoon and is in the hospital."

As Vincenzo's brows knit together, Dino tugged on her arm. She looked down. "What is it?"

"Who's in the hospital?"

"Leon's brother."

"Was he your friend, too?" he asked in all innocence. Both men stared at her till she could scarcely take another breath.

"Yes, he was."

"Oh."

"Dino?" Vincenzo put a hand on his son's shoulder. "We'll go out to the car and wait for Irena while she says goodbye to Signore Simonides." His civil demeanor didn't give away what he was feeling inside.

"I'll be right there," she assured him.

When he'd closed the door behind him, Leon let out a sigh. "I'm sorry, Irena. There's no easy way to handle any of this right."

"Don't worry about it. It's just that the wait for the test has made us both edgy."

"The man's desperately in love with you. Anyone can see that."

For Leon to say such a thing thrilled her; if only her husband had said those words to her. "He's the light of my life. I adore him, and would do anything to prevent him from being hurt."

He shook his head. "Now everything makes sense. For you to let Andreas go the way you did…no histrionics…"

"I'd already fallen for Vincenzo and was ready to break it off with your brother."

Leon's eyes were full of pain. "What a situation for you to be in now."

"Only you would understand how much I want this baby to be Vincenzo's. But if it isn't, I'm going to deal with it the way you did."

She walked over to her desk and got her purse out of the drawer. "Come on. I'll go out to the parking lot with you. There's a little boy and his papa waiting for me."

They rode the private elevator to the ground floor. Before they walked past security at the main door of the building she turned to him. "I can't believe Andreas isn't going to recover so I won't even consider it."

"That makes two of us." Leon gave her another hug. "Deline sends her love."

"Take mine back to her."

While Leon headed for his rental car in one direction, anxious to get back to Athens, she hurried toward the VIP parking in the other. Dino was leaning out the rear window of the Fiat, waiting for her. "Irena!" he called to her with a big smile on his face. It warmed her heart.

She gave him a kiss on the cheek before climbing in the front passenger seat. Vincenzo had leaned across to open the door for her. Without speaking to her, he started the car and they drove away.

"Where is your friend sick?" Dino wanted to know.

"He has a bug." She patted her tummy, a gesture Vincenzo noted. It reminded them both of the baby she was carrying. He translated for his son, who said, *"Che tristezza."*

Yes, it was sad. *"Sì,* Dino. But in time he will get better."

"The point is, will you?" Vincenzo threw out in a gravelly voice.

Leon's visit had brought the question of paternity to the forefront once more. Somehow she had to help get her husband's mind off it. When they pulled up at the back of the apartment, he announced they were going to the park as soon as they changed clothes.

Dino sounded delighted and scrambled out of the car. Irena followed him inside, deciding to put on white shorts and a matching knit top. Because the heat was particularly intense, she tied her hair back at the nape with a white scarf.

When she went back in the living room, she discovered Vincenzo had changed out of his suit into blue shorts and a lighter blue T-shirt, much like the outfit Dino was wearing. One day he would grow up to have the same hard-muscled physique as his father. No woman would be immune to him, either.

The park was just past the church on the same side. When they reached it, there were at least a dozen children playing. Vincenzo opened the duffel bag holding his son's equipment and pulled out a soccer ball.

"Watch me, Irena!"

Dino started kicking it around with his father. Vincenzo was a natural athlete and a natural with children. Pretty soon some other boys joined in. Irena sat in one of the swings, content to have a legitimate reason to look at her striking husband as long as she wanted. His powerful legs fascinated her. She remembered the way they felt entwined with hers.

A fierce ache passed through her body. Irena wished she could make her world perfect, but knowing she couldn't, she started swinging like she did when she was a child. Higher and higher.

"Careful," Vincenzo murmured, catching her midway, swing and all, bringing her to a stop from behind. "Remember the test. This close to the date you don't want to do anything that could cause a complication. If this broke…"

"You're right." She slid out of it and turned to him. "I wasn't thinking."

His gaze took her in, missing nothing from her sandals to the scarf holding her hair back. The little muscle at the corner of his mouth throbbed, revealing emotion held barely in check. "That doesn't surprise me. It isn't every day you hear Simonides is in the hospital."

"Vincenzo—" She lifted beseeching eyes to

him. "I had no idea Leon had flown here. If I'd known, I would have told you."

"I believe you."

She moistened her lips nervously, aware of his scrutiny. Beyond his shoulder she could see Dino playing soccer with the other boys. For the moment the two of them were alone. "He's worried about his brother."

"I can only surmise he doesn't want you to say or do anything that could upset his twin."

For such a brilliant man, she couldn't understand how Vincenzo was so blind to the intensity of her feelings for *him*.

"I told him I wasn't going to worry about anything because I'm planning on *you* being the father. By the time he's recovered, I'll know the test results."

Vincenzo rubbed his lower lip with the pad of his thumb. "And then what?"

"If he's the father, I'll let Leon choose the moment to take the DNA results to him. But I don't want to think about it right now. I want to concentrate on us."

"So do I," he whispered against her lips. On that healing note, Vincenzo turned and called to Dino that they were leaving. He came running over to them, holding his ball. "What are we going to do now?"

She leaned down. "Shall we buy a gelato?"

"At the pool?"

Irena squinted at him. "No. At the *gelateria*."

"Don't you want to go to the pool?"

She didn't understand. "I thought you didn't like to go there."

He nodded his dark head. "Yes, I do."

Her pulse quickened to realize Vincenzo had managed some kind of breakthrough with his son. *"Veramente?"*

"Sì." Dino laughed. "There aren't any sharks in a pool! Everyone knows *that!"*

Overjoyed, she gave him a big hug. "I'm so glad you told me. Now I'll get in the pool with you."

"Fantastico! Let's get our bathing suits on!"

Irena was so happy with this much progress

where his son was concerned, she wanted to hug her husband and never let him go, but the paternity of the baby still clouded their future. If the baby was Andreas's then their family would always be divided. Irena couldn't bear to think about it and so instead she showered all her attention on Dino, the child they had at the moment, pretending that Vincenzo's baby was growing inside of her.

By Sunday night they'd had such a wonderful time playing and swimming, there were tears from Dino at the helipad in Milan. Vincenzo stood outside the open door of the helicopter, but his son was all broken up and refused to get out.

"How come you can't come and get me next weekend, Papa?"

Irena had to clamp down hard on her emotions so they wouldn't show. Next weekend the test would be done and over, and a new chapter of their lives would begin.

"Because one weekend a month your mother

wants you with her. It's all been planned, but we'll see you on Wednesday."

That cheered him up a little. "Okay."

"I'll study all the colors, *professore*," Irena promised. "You can test me to see if I make any mistakes."

A small smile broke the corners of his mouth.

"If she does them all correctly, what will you give her for a reward?" his father asked him.

"Do you like chocolate?"

"I can't live without it."

Dino laughed. It was good to see him leave in a happier mood. *"Ciao."*

"A presto, Dino. Ti amo." She'd wanted to tell him she loved him a long time ago, but until now it hadn't felt like the right moment.

"Ti amo, Irena." That was a first for him, too. He was the sweetest boy in the world. After a quick hug, he turned so his father could grab him.

Once they'd driven away in the limo, she phoned Deline. Since Leon's unexpected visit on Friday, Irena hadn't heard another word. To her disappointment it rang so long, she had to leave a message.

Five minutes later Deline phoned her back. "I'm so sorry I couldn't answer. We've been at the hospital with Andreas."

"How is he?"

"Yesterday they found out he has a rare parasite, but it's treatable. They started him on antibiotics and already his temperature has dropped. He kept down a roll and some juice tonight. If he continues to improve, he'll be able to go home in the next couple of days."

"That's good. Now I've got some wonderful news. Tonight Vincenzo's son told me he loved me."

"Oh, Irena…"

"Dino's going to make the most fabulous big brother for my baby. For the sake of all our sanity, that test can't come soon enough."

"It's only a few days away now. Hang on, Irena."

CHAPTER NINE

THE PERINATOLOGIST DOING the procedure came in the room. He nodded to Vincenzo before approaching Irena. "How are you feeling this morning, Signora Valsecchi?"

"Good. Anxious."

"I'm sure Dr. Santi told you what's going to happen. The ultrasound technician will be working with me. Once I've numbed your belly, I'll insert a long, thin needle. It will pass through the uterus to the placenta where I'll gather a sample of cells. You might feel a little cramping, but the procedure won't take more than twenty-five minutes. Do you have any questions?"

"No."

The doctor was ready to begin. Vincenzo was the one standing in the way of things getting started. He'd never liked the idea of her having this test and preferred to call the whole thing off, but Irena was determined.

He leaned over his wife, who'd drunk the necessary glass of water an hour ago and had been prepped for the ultrasound. "If you need me, I'll be as close as the reception room."

"I know." Her velvety-brown eyes pleaded with him to understand why she was doing this. But this kind of courage he didn't admire. It not only constituted a certain risk to the baby, but it also placed her in physical as well as emotional jeopardy. The thought of anything going wrong—or, God forbid, losing her—was incomprehensible to him.

She gripped his forearm as if sensing his inner turmoil. "It's going to be all right."

To the depths of his soul Vincenzo wanted, *had* to believe it. He kissed her lips before wheeling out of the room.

A month ago he'd had an inward struggle over the baby's paternity, but having just left his wife, he realized she was the only thing that mattered to him. So what if the baby wasn't his? He just wanted the baby and his wife to be safe and well.

Having met her, he was a changed man. Fulfilled on every level. As long as he had her, any other frustration or disappointment he could deal with.

Needing something to do, he headed over to the alcove to get himself coffee out of the machine. After draining the cup, he walked down the hallway to the lab and approached the fiftyish-looking female receptionist.

"Is there someone in charge I could speak to?"

One brown brow lifted. "I've worked here thirty years."

Her response would have amused him if he wasn't in such turmoil over Irena and the baby. "My wife's having a Chorionic Villi Sampling done as we speak to determine the paternity of her baby. When I came in to give a sample of my cheek tissue, the technician said the results for both of us would be ready in about ten days."

"But you want to know *now*."

Ehi. She'd been here thirty years all right. Vincenzo nodded.

"If you want to pay more money, you can know the results as soon as tomorrow."

His head reeled before he reached for his wallet.

She laughed. "Not to me. To the cashier down the hall. Everything's legal here."

He took a deep breath. He should have felt like a fool, but he didn't. "What's the protocol? Do I phone the lab?"

"You look like you're dying, so I'll call you by noon." She pushed a notepad through the window opening.

Vincenzo wrote down his and Irena's names and cell phone numbers and passed it back. "If you weren't sitting on the other side of the glass, I'd kiss you, signora."

"Signorina Loti. If there weren't any glass, I'd let you."

"Grazie," he said with heartfelt emotion before finding the cashier. After producing a credit card, he went back to the reception room.

He wouldn't tell Irena what he'd done. If anything, it could bring on more anxiety. Her health was all that mattered to him. Dr. Santi said to give her three days to recover. There could be some bleeding, which was normal. Plenty of bed rest, no strenuous exercise.

Once he'd heard from the lab, he'd tell her, of course. But until then, he'd wait out the next twenty-four hours without her knowing she'd be getting an answer much sooner than she'd expected.

"Signore Valsecchi?"

Infinitely relieved to hear his name called, Vincenzo followed the nurse back to Irena's room. When he went inside, she was up and dressed, sitting in a wheelchair, looking too good for someone who'd just gone through such an uncomfortable experience.

He leaned down to press a brief kiss to the mouth he craved. "How are you feeling?"

"I'm really fine." *Grazie a dio.* "You've probably been going crazy waiting."

His pulse sped up knowing he needed to keep the truth from her a little longer. "I have, but everything's okay now that I can take you home."

"She's ready," the nurse said, putting a sheet of instructions in Irena's hands. "If you want to wheel her out, I'll accompany you to the entry and wait while you bring your car around."

Before long he'd helped her into the car and they drove out of the hospital parking lot. He looked over at her. "Are you hungry? Thirsty? I'll be happy to stop and get you anything you want."

"Thank you, but let's just go home."

He reached out to grasp the hand closest to him. "That's what I want, too."

She heaved an emotional sigh he felt go through him. "I'm glad it's over, Vincenzo."

"So am I. We will know soon and then we

can start living our life. Are you feeling any discomfort yet?"

"No. There was a little stinging around the needle, but that soon left. I feel amazingly normal."

"You look it, but don't be deceived. You heard what Dr. Santi said."

"I know. I'll take it easy."

"We both will. I'll feed you grapes while you recite your conjugations for me. By the time we go for Dino on Wednesday, he'll be so impressed with how much progress you've made, he'll ask me to buy you some chocolate bocci balls."

"One of those sounds good."

He rubbed her fingers before letting them go. "You're not pretending? You really do feel okay?"

"Yes. The only problem now is the ten-day wait. By then Andreas—"

"By then Simonides could have discovered about the baby, yes…" he cut in, trying not to sound harsh. "We'll deal with it when the time comes...." His voice trailed.

"I'm sorry, Vincenzo. I don't mean to keep bringing him up."

"Don't apologize. If he is the father then he is going to be a fact of life like Mila." If it were true, somehow Vincenzo would have to learn to deal with it, but in his heart he still hoped...

When they reached Riomaggiore and he pulled up behind the apartment, she undid the seat belt and started to get out of the car, but he caught her arm. "You've just had surgery. Let me help you."

"I was only going to walk in the house. That's not strenuous."

Upset, he levered himself from the seat and went around to her side. "Whether it is or not, I'm carrying you inside."

She looped her arms around his neck. "You do too much for me. I feel like a fraud."

"Feel any way you like," he bit out. "I want to take care of you."

Irena kissed his cheek. "That's all you ever

do. I'm the luckiest woman in the world." Tears filled her eyes at his gentleness.

He swept her through the front door, hoping she still felt that way after hearing the test results. "Do you feel like bed, or the couch?"

"The couch, but first I need to use the bathroom."

Vincenzo lowered her to the floor. "I'll make us something to eat."

"That sounds perfect." She gave him another kiss and started down the hall.

When she'd shut the door, he hurried out to the kitchen. His gaze caught sight of the homemade volcano sitting on the counter. She'd helped Dino make it on Wednesday. After several attempts, it finally blew and was such a huge success, his son wanted to do it again next week.

He pulled the food out of the fridge with more force than necessary. In his gut he wanted the baby she carried to be his; he wanted their family to be together always, without the fear of visitation always hanging over them. Once the results were in and Vincenzo had the truth staring him in the face, maybe then he could let everything go. But right now he felt like that volcano sitting there ready to go off.

Irena woke up the next morning with a start. It was almost ten. She'd been so nervous the night before, she'd stayed up late with Vincenzo watching a couple of old movies until fatigue took over.

To her surprise she'd slept soundly, but now that she was awake, she remembered the procedure and hurried to the bathroom.

She could have cried out with relief because there was no leak of amniotic fluid and only a mere spot of blood.

After taking a quick shower, she brushed her hair and put on lipstick, wanting to look good for her husband. Next came a pair of jeans he hadn't seen her in before. She toned them with a sleeveless top in a café-au-lait color with white trim around the armholes and neck.

When she entered the kitchen, Vincenzo had

already fixed their breakfast. His anxious gaze searched hers. "You're up!"

"Forgive me for sleeping in."

"Forgive you—" he cried out in exasperation. "You needed it. But for the last three hours I have to admit I've been checking on you every ten minutes, worrying you might not be breathing." Emotion had darkened his eyes to a deeper blue.

"I'm sorry." Since driving her home from the hospital, it was as if he was in a continual state of agitation, waiting to hear the worst.

"What's the verdict?"

"So far, perfect!" She smiled to reassure him, but he wasn't convinced. "Vincenzo—more than twelve hours have already passed. Dr. Santi said they were the most crucial, but everything's fine. Only the merest trace of blood, nothing else. If I were going to miscarry, there'd be more signs."

"No pain?"

"None!" She spread her hands the way he did, hoping he'd see she was even learning Italian gestures, but by his expression they were wasted on him.

"You wouldn't lie to me—" His voice sounded unsteady.

"Why would I do that?" She took a step closer, not understanding this new side of him. His vulnerability was a complete revelation to her. No one seeing him like this would believe he was the confident, brilliant, in-charge Duke of La Spezia who was already making radically new changes at the Valsecchi corporation.

"You know everything there is to know about me. You *have* to know it! Believe me, if I were cramping and miserable, I would tell you, Vincenzo." She could see that something deeper was bothering him and that he wanted to talk to her about something so she tried to lighten the mood, hoping to get Vincenzo talking to her.

"Look, Vincenzo, if I was in any kind of pain do you think I would be wearing jeans like this for you? Do you remember how you once dared me to buy a pair like this when I came to Italy the first time?"

She modeled them in front of him, like she was on the runway of a fashion designer's shop. "Take a good look now because I won't be able to stuff myself into them much longer, not when the baby comes."

His jaw hardened, but his eyes watched every movement. That had to mean something. Now that the test was over and she hadn't miscarried, was Vincenzo worried about their future? Did he regret marrying her for the baby's sake? Irena continued, determined to find out what had caused her husband's sudden darkened mood.

"If you don't remember, *I* do. We were walking along the hiking path to Manarola behind a knockout Italian girl and her boyfriend. You challenged me to get a pair like she was wearing. As far as I was concerned, she might as well have not been wearing them for all the good they did her."

"That's a matter of opinion," he muttered,

but she heard him. At least he was listening. It gave her the courage to go on.

"I told you a lady didn't pour herself into such an outfit. You said a man didn't always want the woman he loved to be dressed like a business-woman. Maybe you don't remember, but you said a lot of things like that to me when we first met.

"When you told me you liked my height be-cause there was more of me to grab hold of, I expected you to grab me. I *wanted* you to do it, and you *knew* it! But you teased me by not giving me what I wanted and drove me insane with wanting!"

That nerve at the corner of his mouth was throbbing again. "You were toying with me."

She put her hands on her hips, furious that she couldn't seem to get through to him. What was going on here? "I would never toy with you, Vincenzo."

"Then why did you come back to Italy? The truth now!"

"The truth?" she cried, baffled by his question.

"You *know* why, Vincenzo." She went to him and placed her hand against his strong arm. He twitched, but did not pull away. Irena knew that she had to convince her husband of her true feelings for him. For so long she had been avoiding talking to him about how she felt, but with the test now behind them and their future ahead it suddenly felt liberating to say it.

"Vincenzo, the night I went to bed with you was the night I knew I'd fallen completely and irrevocably in love with a man for the first time in my life. That man was *you!* You were right about dreams, Vincenzo. You were right about everything! I did have a dream of being married to Andreas, but that's all it was, a silly dream, a fantasy.

"With hindsight I can see our relationship always lacked the fire, though we seemed like the perfect couple. Everyone thought so. But we were never true lovers and never felt it in our hearts. Andreas only ever made love to me twice."

"I don't believe you." His response sounded almost savage.

"Believe it. Both times were disappointing."

If anything, her husband seemed to pale with the revelation.

"Then I met you. Vincenzo Antonello. The most arrogant, gorgeous, impossible Italian male in existence with his beat-up car and his attitude that said to hell with the world. *Sì, signore*—" She nodded because he wasn't making any sound.

"You were that bad. Worse even. We were anything but the perfect couple. A mismatch in every way, shape and form. But by that first night, I felt like I'd met the lover I wanted to spend the rest of my life with. Every day after that I fell more and more in love even though you never said you were in love with me."

She took a fortifying breath. "I didn't want to leave you when it was time to go home, Vincenzo. I'd forgotten all about Andreas. I stayed in Italy three days longer than I should have because I couldn't bear to leave. I knew I had to tell Andreas about you, that I was in love with *you*. There was no way I could have gone back to him. My heart was with you, darling, and he had to be told.

"But he'd already fallen for Gabi so I never did get the chance to tell him about us. He was in a hurry when he came to my house and so full of his feelings for her, he did all the talking. It was a revelation to hear him pour out his heart. For once he was actually communicating to me, and everything he said I could relate to because love had happened to me, too."

Vincenzo still refused to speak, but Irena, filled with a courage she didn't know she had, continued. She knew that this was make-or-break for them—Vincenzo had to know her true feelings; she couldn't lose him now, after all they had been through!

"I gave up my job at the newspaper and made plans to fly back to you, Vincenzo, but I started feeling sick and the nausea was bad enough that I staycd in Athens to see a doctor. You know the rest of the story.

"So here we are, my love, together and married with a baby on the way. At first I feared that Andreas might be the father, but I can't worry about that any longer. He chose his path and I chose mine. It's in the past. My life is with you and Dino and the baby. We'll deal with whatever happens. All I know is, I couldn't live without you now."

A silence settled around them whilst Irena waited for Vincenzo to respond. He was staring at the floor and for a horrifying moment Irena believed that the marriage might be at an end. Perhaps this had been too much for Vincenzo to deal with? Then the silence was interrupted by the ringing of the telephone. Both of them seemed surprised by the intrusion, drawing them out of their solitude.

Vincenzo automatically picked it up from the counter, his eyes riveted on her mouth. *"Prego? Buongiorno. Sì. Momento."* Vincenzo handed the phone to her. "It's Dr. Santi calling to ask how you're doing."

"Oh—" She put it to her ear. *"Buongiorno, Dr. Santi."*

"How are you today?"

"Wonderful. Only a little blood. Nothing else. No cramps."

"Ah…that's what I was hoping to hear. Are you ready for some more good news?"

Her heart pounded harder. "Yes. Of course."

"While you were having the procedure done yesterday, your husband had a conversation with the head of the lab. He asked if they would rush the preliminary report. I have the results in my hand. Both your doctors were wise not to tell you anything definitive in the beginning. The baby is your husband's."

Irena thought she was going to collapse with joy. Her heart felt like it was flying on wings. "Oh, Dr. Santi—" Tears gushed from her eyes.

"What's wrong?" Vincenzo cried in agony.

"I'll see you in three weeks for your next appointment."

He rushed around the counter and caught her in his arms. "Tell me what's the matter, *innamorta*."

She grabbed his face between her hands. "Not a single, solitary thing. Vincenzo, *you're* the father of our baby! *You're* the one who made me pregnant. This is our baby, yours and mine."

"*Irena*—" He covered her face with kisses, unable to stop. "Our baby?"

"Yes, *mia amore. Ti amo.* If I didn't say that right, I don't care. I love you, Vincenzo. That night we made love, we created a family. *Our* family. Oh, darling—"

He started kissing her and couldn't stop. She didn't want him to stop. Before she knew it they were on the bed in his bedroom, entwined while they poured out their love. He hadn't brought her in here since the night their baby was conceived. From now on this was where she intended to sleep. In his arms.

"I know I have to slow down," he whispered on a ragged breath. "The doctor said three days. We've got two more to go before we know it's safe. How am I going to make it? You're going to have to help me." He kissed her long and deep. *"Agape mou."*

Her body quickened. "You just said you loved me in Greek."

"I've never told another woman I was in love with her, but I wanted to tell you that first night. I wanted you to hear me tell you in your own language first. Don't you think it's time I learned it? We want our son or daughter to be equally at home in both languages, don't we?"

"Oh, yes—" she cried softly, covering his face with kisses. "I'll teach you and Dino together. We're going to have the most wonderful life!" Her emotions burst their bonds and she broke down in joyful sobs. "I love you, Vincenzo. I love our baby. I love Dino. No woman in this world could be as happy as I am at this moment."

"Nor man," he said against her lips. "Today feels like the first day of life. Our lives." Vincenzo became serious for a moment as he looked deep into her eyes. "Irena, I'm sorry I was so distant before. The thought of anything happening to you or the baby filled me with fear. You have both become the most important things in my life and to lose you... I don't think I could have coped. I also feared that if the baby was Andreas's then the turmoil of visitation might destroy you. I felt helpless, for the first time in my life." He kissed her then and the kiss grew into something deep and intense, robbing them both of their breath.

"That's why we can't stay on this bed any longer. I don't trust myself not to make love to you."

"I don't want to do anything to hurt our baby, either, so I'll get up and we'll go in the other room to enjoy that fabulous breakfast you made in celebration of this incredible day."

"And while we do that—" He nibbled on her earlobe. "You phone the one person who needs to know our news. Then we're going to relax around here all day while I feed you chocolate bocci balls and we think up names."

"That sounds wonderful." She kissed his hard jaw. "And start planning a nursery."

"Did I tell you Papa has insisted that we live at the palazzo with him and Silviana? I agreed at the time to placate him, but have no intention of following through."

Irena shifted positions so she could look down at him. "Why not?"

He traced the line of her mouth with his finger. "You know why, *bellisima*. We're both free spirits. I want our baby to be one, too, and I'm doing all I can to turn Dino into one."

"But what would it hurt for a little while? We'll keep the apartment and go back and forth. Your father might not have long left. Don't you think he made it a demand because deep down he was afraid you'd never come of your own free will?"

She kissed his mouth. "I think it's his way of trying to make up for the years you were estranged. Dino likes it there. Would it be so impossible for you? I know you love your father."

His hand tightened in her hair. Emotion had turned his eyes a deeper blue. "What did I ever do to deserve you?"

"I've asked that same question about you since the day you took me on that picnic. Beneath the tower you pelted me with flowers, like a knight might have done to his lady centuries before. I felt enchanted. You had enchanted me. Now that I'm carrying your baby, nothing could ever thrill me more. I don't care where we live as long as I'm with you."

"Irena—" He crushed her to him one more time. With reluctance he finally got to his feet and pulled her up with him. Arm in arm they left the bedroom and walked to the kitchen. Vincenzo handed her the phone.

Shaking with excitement, she called her friend. It was Saturday morning. She could be in Athens or on Milos. *Pick up, Deline.*

After six rings: "Irena?"

She put it on speaker for Vincenzo. "Yes! Where are you?"

"On the boat with Leon and the twins."

"Good. I have news you're both going to want to hear." Irena's gaze had fused with her husband's. His eyes were suspiciously bright. "Vincenzo is the father of my baby!"

Her friend's cry of happiness was so loud, it hurt their eardrums. She was already shouting the news to Leon.

Irena could hardly talk she was so full of emotion. "We're expecting a little Valescchi in about six and a half months. You'll have to come to La Spezia when we have it christened at the church. You'll stay at the palazzo with us, of course. Love you. *Ciao* for now."

She clicked off before clutching Vincenzo to her. "I love you. I love you so much you're going to get sick of hearing me say it."

"I'll get sick if you don't. Hand me the phone. I've got a phone call I'd like to make."

Irena was trembling so hard, she had to cling to her husband while he pressed the digits. He put the phone on speaker and all of a sudden she could hear her mother answer. Vincenzo asked her to put Irena's father on, too. He joined within seconds.

"We've been wondering when we'd hear from you two."

Vincenzo smiled down at her. "As you know, your brilliant daughter has been helping me get the company back on track, but we've taken three days off to celebrate and wanted you to do it with us since you're going to be grandparents in about six and half months."

"You're pregnant? Our little girl's pregnant!" her mother almost shrieked with joy.

"This is wonderful." Her father sounded all choked up.

"Irena will call you later and give you all the details. Right now we have to inform my father and his wife."

"Another little duke perhaps?"

"Or duchess," Irena teased, knowing full well how Vincenzo felt about that, but it never hurt to placate the parents while they were so delighted. "But don't you dare print anything yet!"

Her father roared with laughter before clicking off.

After Vincenzo hung up, she kissed him hungrily once more. "You're going to be the most wonderful father. Do you want a boy or a girl? Do you realize in all this time we haven't talked about that?"

He'd buried his face in her hair. "I don't care."

"Neither do I."

"Give me your mouth, Irena. It's life to me."

"I will after we call your father. Let me tell him. We've begun to be friends."

"I know. He's secretly crazy about you, but then, so am I. I'm hopelessly in love, *squisita*."

Six and a half months later

"The head's crowning, Irena. Your baby's coming. One more push. You can do it."

"Come on, *cara*," Vincenzo coached her.

Another push and she heard a gurgling sound

followed by an infant cry. She watched Dr. Santi hold the baby up before laying it across her stomach.

"You've got a sweet little girl here. She has a perfect set of lungs. Go ahead and cut the cord, Vincenzo."

Her husband, in gown and mask, appeared to have nerves of steel as he did the honors, but she knew deep inside he'd been terrified of anything going wrong.

In another minute the pediatrician took over and examined her. Once he'd cleaned her up, he put her in a blanket for Irena to hold. He glanced at Vincenzo. "She has her papa's eyes. They're already turning blue."

Irena sent her husband a secret smile. No one could know what those words meant to Vincenzo. He really was her papa.

"Everything looks terrific, Signora Valsecchi. She's eight pounds, and nineteen and a half inches long."

"Oh, darling—I can't believe she's here! Our baby at last!" Tears streamed down her face.

When she looked up at him again, his were wet, too.

"She's perfect," he whispered in absolute wonder.

"She has the Valsecchi profile, just like Dino's."

"She's gorgeous, just like her mother."

"It doesn't seem possible we're holding our own baby." Irena couldn't believe how exquisite she was. She had tiny, feminine fingers and nails. But Irena saw other parts that belonged to her handsome daddy in the shape of her kissable mouth and head.

Vincenzo let out the joyous, uninhibited laughter of a happy, relieved father who no longer had to worry that the test done at ten weeks had harmed their baby in any way. The last shadow hanging over their marriage had just gone poof!

Guilio poked his head inside the door of her room, eyeing her with a smile. "Can people come in yet? Dino can't wait much longer."

"Of course," Irena told him, but Vincenzo

asked his father to wait outside for a few more minutes. He was still examining their daughter with infinite care.

"You can't ask him to wait forever, darling."

"There's a whole crowd out there, Irena," he grumbled. "I don't think it's a good idea to let everyone in yet."

"But they want to see our baby."

"So do I," he said a little gruffly. "I'll let them in when I think you and Alessandra are ready and not before."

Whoa. She'd never seen him quite like this before. Another new aspect for her to love.

He pulled his mask off. "Are you all right? After what you've been through, I don't know how you could be so calm and look so beautiful." He brushed her lips with his own.

Irena adored this marvelous husband and kissed him back more thoroughly than he'd expected. "I'm not a fragile invalid," she whispered.

"Dr. Santi has put me in a bad mood. She said we have to wait six weeks."

"But I feel so wonderful I don't see why we'll have to wait that long. Do you?" The hungry kiss she gave him seemed to have done the trick. It was one of her wifely secrets that always worked because it had managed to put a gleam in his eye. For a little while she'd feared it had disappeared for a long time.

"We'll see," he teased. Then more forcefully said, "I love you. You know that. If anything had happened to you…"

"But it didn't. Remember that I love you. And let Dino in. He's been waiting and waiting with your father. I don't ever want him to feel excluded."

"Neither do I." He walked over to the door. "One at a time, everyone. Dino first."

Taking hold of his father's hand, he walked gingerly toward the bed. She put out her arm. "I'm so glad you're here, Dino. I've missed you. Sit down in that chair and your father will let you hold your new little sister."

After Vincenzo took their precious bundle

and placed it in his boy's lap, Dino studied the baby's face and hands for a long time.

"What do you think?" his father asked.

"She doesn't have any hair."

Irena laughed. "She will. My mother told me I was bald when I was born. Look at me now."

That brought a smile to his face. "Papa says he loves your hair."

"Is that true, *esposo mio?*"

For the first time since she'd known him, she believed he actually blushed.

"How soon will Alessandra be able to walk?"

Irena had to think. "Maybe a year."

"Nine months!" Vincenzo said in his authoritative voice.

She shot her husband a mischievous smile. "Do you know something that I don't?"

"She's a Valsecchi and therefore is already advanced for her age."

"Was I advanced, Papa?"

"Naturally," sounded another voice. Guilio and Silviana had come into the room. The old man's eyes were glazed with moisture as he bent over the newest arrival to the Valsecchi clan. He eventually lifted his head. Looking from one to the other he said, "You two do good work, both in and out of the office."

That was one compliment Irena would always hug to her heart. He patted Vincenzo on the shoulder. With a gorgeous nursery all decked out at the palazzo, the two of them had come a long way since the end of their estrangement.

"For a man who never jokes, that was pretty good, Papa."

"Do you want to hold her, Grandpa?"

"No, no. You're doing a fine job."

"Darling?" Irena whispered to her husband. "I can hear my mother's voice outside. I was afraid their flight would never get here. Tell them to come in."

The next few minutes were a blur as Irena's parents swept in the room with gifts and hugs. Both were beaming. They adored Vincenzo and Dino. Now they were ready to shower their love on their only grandchild.

Alessandra got passed around so much, it was worrying Vincenzo again, but she begged him to let his uncles and aunts have their turn first. Soon the whole place sounded like a party until the nurse came in and ushered everyone out.

Irena had to admit she was exhausted. She squeezed Dino's hand and asked him to come back later. The next time she awakened, the nurse came in with the baby to help her start nursing. Then she fell back to sleep again.

This time when she opened her eyes, she was surrounded by at least a dozen bouquets placed on countertops and carts. Just as she was wondering where her husband had gone, Vincenzo walked in the room with a vase of three dozen long-stemmed red roses. She let out a cry. "They're glorious!"

"Just like you." He set them on her side table.

"Vincenzo—"

"Quick, before our baby comes back." He kissed her long and passionately. When he finally lifted his head he said, "I've been need-ing that."

"So have I. Have you been with our daugh-ter?"

"I spent part of the time in the nursery so I could bathe her. Dino watched through the glass. Afterward I took him for a meal in the cafeteria."

"Good. What does he think about all this?"

"He says he's going to tell his mother he has to come here more often because you're going to need help with the baby. He loves you, *tesoro.*"

"The feeling's mutual."

"Dino's staying with my father and Silviana tonight so I can be here with you. Tomorrow if you're released, we'll all go home together."

"I'm too happy." She glanced around. "I can't believe all these flowers. Such an outpouring. Even from Fabbio."

"You've made a lot of friends and won him over too since you became my cochair. Later I'll give you the cards to look at, but there's a

sealed note meant for you in one of the bouquets. Would you like to read it now?"

Obviously it was important to her husband
that she did. As tired as she was she said yes.

He handed her the envelope. Inside was a
florist card that read Congratulations from
Andreas and Gabi. She broke the seal on the
paper and opened it. Andreas had penned a
message.

Dear Irena—

When Leon told me you'd married the
man of your dreams and were expecting
his child, I realized that the same thing that
happened to me had happened to you. Fate
had something wonderful in store for both
of us that neither of us could have foreseen
when we started down our path together. If
you're feeling like I am, you've thrown off
any residual guilt for unintentional hurt we
might have caused each other.

Gabi and I are expecting a baby in three
months. My joy is beyond words. What

makes me so happy is that I know yours is, too. I'm anxious to meet Vincenzo. He has to be someone exceptional to have won you heart and soul. In the years to come, our paths will cross often, something I'll always look forward to.

Andreas.

Wordlessly, she handed it to her husband for him to read. She watched him pore over it several times. After a few minutes she heard him say, "He's not called the great Simonides for nothing, is he?"

She stared at the man she worshipped. "I love you, Vincenzo," she cried emotionally. "Come here." ١٢١

MILLS & BOON PUBLISH EIGHT LARGE PRINT TITLES A MONTH. THESE ARE THE EIGHT TITLES FOR FEBRUARY 2011.

C3

THE RELUCTANT SURRENDER
Penny Jordan

SHAMEFUL SECRET, SHOTGUN WEDDING
Sharon Kendrick

THE VIRGIN'S CHOICE
Jennie Lucas

SCANDAL: UNCLAIMED LOVE-CHILD
Melanie Milburne

ACCIDENTALLY PREGNANT!
Rebecca Winters

STAR-CROSSED SWEETHEARTS
Jackie Braun

A MIRACLE FOR HIS SECRET SON
Barbara Hannay

PROUD RANCHER, PRECIOUS BUNDLE
Donna Alward

MILLS & BOON PUBLISH EIGHT LARGE PRINT TITLES A MONTH. THESE ARE THE EIGHT TITLES FOR MARCH 2011.

THE DUTIFUL WIFE
Penny Jordan

HIS CHRISTMAS VIRGIN
Carole Mortimer

PUBLIC MARRIAGE, PRIVATE SECRETS
Helen Bianchin

FORBIDDEN OR FOR BEDDING?
Julia James

CHRISTMAS WITH HER BOSS
Marion Lennox

FIREFIGHTER'S DOORSTEP BABY
Barbara McMahon

DADDY BY CHRISTMAS
Patricia Thayer

CHRISTMAS MAGIC ON THE MOUNTAIN
Melissa McClone